THE LOVE MONSTER

The Love Monster

MISSY MARSTON

ESPLANADE
Books

THE FICTION SERIES AT VÉHICULE PRESS

Published with the generous assistance of The Canada Council for the Arts and the Canada Book Fund of the Department of Canadian Heritage.

Esplanade Books editor: Andrew Steinmetz
Cover design: David Drummond
Photograph of author: Dan Ziemkievicz
Set in Adobe Minion by Simon Garamond
Printed by Marquis Book Printing Inc.

Copyright © Missy Marston 2012
Dépôt légal, Bibliothèque nationale du Québec and the National Library of Canada, second trimester 2012
All rights reserved.

LIBRARY AND ARCHIVES CANADA CATALOGUING IN PUBLICATION

Marston, Missy
The love monster / Missy Marston.
ISBN: 978-1-55065-326-7
I. Title.

PS8626.A7677L68 2012   C813'.6   C2012-901917-8

Published by Véhicule Press, Montréal, Québec, Canada
www.vehiculepress.com

Distribution in Canada by LitDistCo
www.litdistco.ca

Distribution in the U.S. by Independent Publishers Group
www.ipgbook.com

Printed in Canada on FSC certified paper.

For Peter, Lake and Silas

Prologue

Nothing will ever be the same

AFTER YOU NOTICE THE FIRST wrinkle or grey hair, after your husband or wife or child leaves forever, after you have been abducted by aliens, nothing will ever be the same. Everyone knows this. Everything will fall apart, will come undone, will break ranks and head for the hills.

After a heart attack, a car accident, a hurricane, murder or suicide, nothing will ever be the same. Things break into so many pieces you wonder how it all fit together in the first place. And you know damn well it will not be put back together.

After the house burns down, after the crop is blighted, after the train jumps the tracks and goes tearing up the turf, when you find yourself standing alone, staring at the smouldering twisted wreckage, you have to build something new. A Frankenstein version of yourself, your life. A crazy nasty silly monster puppet. It will not be pretty. It is not what you had planned. But if you are lucky, it will be a big strong brute. A big strong brute full of sweet monster love. And live, pumping blood.

That's what this story is about.

One

Margaret Atwood and the sad decline

HER NAME IS MARGARET ATWOOD. That's right. She is no relation, bears no resemblance, has no literary ambitions; she simply bears the same damn good name. She has explained all these things to shop clerks and bank tellers and office nurses throughout her adult life. Yet they persist.

In fact, her name is Margaret H. Atwood, but don't ask her about the *H*. Really. Never ask.

Margaret H. Atwood is thirty-five. She is thirty-five years old and she can feel herself getting thicker around the middle. She feels thick around the middle like an old battle-axe, the kind that bustles around in a fat column of tight wool skirt-suit. Recently, she has done an inventory and found the following to be true. Her eyes are much less surprised-looking than they once were; they are getting hooded and bored-looking. There is the faintest hint of jowl at her jaw line, a barely perceptible crinkling between her breasts. Most disconcerting of all, there is a single, recurring whisker in the middle of her chin. She has pulled it out, with increasing rage, ten times. She will pull it out again, goddamn it.

This realization – that every single part of her, no matter what course of action she takes, will get uglier over time, that the process is inevitable and unstoppable – has been crushing. She understands that to be concerned with such things may be viewed as superficial, that it may somehow be a betrayal of the sisterhood of women, a giving in to the tyranny of 'prescribed beauty' and so on. And so forth. She understands that some would argue that aging is beautiful. She has seen the smarmy television commercial in which the serene voice-over claims to *want* laugh lines. *Growing old is good* is the tagline. It makes her want to kick the television until it all goes away.

Margaret understands, too, that to complain about these things is to risk the outrage of all those who are older than her, those who may be looking wistfully at their thirties (or forties or fifties) in the way she is now looking back at her twenties. She sympathizes. She maintains, however, that a person must be allowed a moment of fury when this terrible truth first settles in, when it first becomes evident that no one will stay the same forever, that every single person will sink and wrinkle and shift and undo. It seems to her unspeakably sad.

And, yes, she knows that both those older than her and those younger than her may find her concerns trivial, laughable. This does not help, does not lend perspective. It does not make her laugh.

She concedes that her unseemly and unforeseen fretting over the physical, over this decaying, disposable human suit we all wear is unforgivably vain. She knows that, in this way and several others, she is very likely a bad person. Her heart is surely very small.

The smaller and faster the heart, the shorter the lifespan

ALSO, LIKE EVERYONE ELSE, she will die. Not immediately, but eventually. This is not news, really. Not news exactly but a preposterous giggle-inducing rumour that gains grim credence with time. Time that accelerates, gains mass and hurtles forward through space. Someone once told Margaret that every year is shorter than the last. She finds this, alarmingly, to be true.

It must also be true that many before her who have had the luxury to think such thoughts have thought them and have found a way through. They have picked themselves up, dusted themselves off and trudged or skipped at steadily increasing speed toward death. She wonders, really, how much she cares about death if she is honest. Is death so bad? Might it be a relief? Likely not. Likely it is nothing at all and probably it is just fine. Obviously: nobody knows. But everybody knows what aging is. Aging is what takes a perfectly nice-looking young woman and turns her into Ed Fucking Asner.

Margaret is not considering any kind of plastic surgery, injection or peel. She is not even considering going to the gym. In truth she does not want to be younger. She would not go back in time at gunpoint. It has seemed, with the exception of a few (admittedly large) glitches, that every step away from childhood has been a step in the right direction. She is simply allowing this revelation about decay, descent and death to inform her decision making.

Now that she is alone, now that Brian is out of her hair and she has time on her hands, she is giving the whole matter a serious thinking-through.

She is reminded often of a nature documentary she once watched on television that related lifespan to the heart rate and size of animals. The theory went that all creatures (with hearts) were allotted roughly the same number of heartbeats and, barring the many possible intervening disasters that can end a life, when they reach the magic number (say 273 million) their life will be over. The machine will have run its course. The variety of natural lifespans could, therefore, be attributed to the various sizes and speeds of hearts: the tiny mile-a-minute heart of a mouse might use up its allotment of beats before lunch time, while the elephant's giant heart will squeeze out a single, massive drumbeat sometime between now and next Tuesday, if it so chooses.

Margaret, a mid-sized animal, wonders what number she is on, how many beats are behind her and how many are ahead. She remembers that Neil Armstrong is rumoured to have had, in his prime, the slowest recorded heart rate of any healthy adult human. Though his title is disputed. Apparently, in the seventies, a yogi named Satyamurti stopped his heart for seven full days.

Seven days. One week. Not one single heartbeat. Or so the story goes.

Satyamurti allowed himself to be hooked up to an ECG, buried himself in a pit in the ground and, through deep meditation, slowed his breathing until the machine registered no heartbeat at all. A straight line dragged across seven days of paper, spooling out onto the ground. Witnesses were understandably concerned. They were certain he was dead. But his disciples would allow no interference, would not dig him up until the exercise was finished and, about half an hour before the yogi was scheduled to be exhumed, the machine stuttered into motion, tracing the familiar skyline of a regular human heartbeat.

When the pit was opened, the yogi smiled up at them, cold and thin and stiff, not only presumably having won some kind of bet, but likely having added a week to his very peculiar life.

It seems absolutely reasonable to Margaret that Neil Armstrong woud have a slow heartbeat, fine figure of a man that he is. Everybody knows that astronauts are subjected to rigorous physical training. It is also possible, she thinks, that the heart would not have to work quite so hard at pumping blood when released from gravity, as an astronaut would be now and again. In any event, Mr. Armstrong must be close to eighty years old now and seems to be doing just fine. He and his slow heart seem, from all appearances, to have many happy years ahead of them.

The yogi is less convincing. Margaret imagines him giggling to himself in the dark as he peels the electrodes off his chest and sticks them to the dirt floor.

Even if she could believe that it were possible, to take control and slow her heart down enough to make some kind of difference in the length of her so-called life, would she bother? Probably not.

Besides, neither the astronaut nor the yogi seems like a reasonable role model. She doubts she is cut out for either lifestyle.

So, go ahead, Heart, run your course.

Come whenever you want, Death, I'm not going anywhere.

Going anywhere

HE KNEW HOW TO PICK his moments, she'll give him that. A regular Tuesday night, 11:30 p.m., Margaret's eyes were burning with fatigue, her head pounding. She had been so close – her teeth brushed, wearing what passed for pyjamas these days (a large, only slightly stained t-shirt, a pair of shorts), padding toward the marital bed – when she had been apprehended. Brian had taken her hand and led her to the living room; he had put his hands on her shoulders and pushed down until her baggy, old shorts touched the couch.

Margaret stares at her husband while he searches for words.

"Brian, *what*? What is it?"

Brian turns his back to her, puts his face in his hands. The lights are too bright in the living room, the shadows stark. The absurd thought crosses Margaret's mind that she wishes she looked better, that she were at least wearing a bra. Her knees are starting to tremble.

Still looking away, he says, "You know I love you."

She wants to stop him. She raises her hands, palms toward him, turns her head to the side.

"It just isn't fair. It isn't fair to you, Margaret."

"Brian, don't." She is getting up from the couch now, shaking her head, walking toward the bedroom.

"Margaret, I'm sorry."

She is stopped now, looking at her bare feet. She does not want to hear another word. But out they come, no less a knife in the heart, no less devastating for being as hackneyed as any words could possibly be: "I'm in love with someone else."

Bastard. It doesn't even sound like he means it. It sounds rehearsed and hollow.

Margaret heads for the bedroom, not wanting to talk, not wanting to catch his eye with hers. She is afraid she will slap him. She wants to kill him with her bare hands.

"I'm serious, Margaret." He is walking after her. "Margaret, be reasonable."

She hates being spoken to like this, like a child. She stops and turns. He looks annoyed and indulgent at the same time; it makes for a singularly unbecoming facial expression in her opinion. She wants so badly to stop him from speaking, to stop him from *being*. She is so tired of him. How did they do it? They have quietly grown to hate each other while loving each other and saying neither thing out loud for so long.

And now it is ruined. Now he is leaving and she can't wait for him to go. He is staring at her, reddening, waiting for something to be said.

"Fuck it. I'm just going to go now."

She trails him as he leaves the bedroom and walks through the living room to the front hall closet where he produces, like a rabbit from a hat, an already-packed suitcase. She thinks, I will never be able to open that closet again without remembering this moment, that stupid suitcase, this sickening night.

And then it hits her: she will not be able to continue living in this house. She knows what will happen after he leaves. This place will feel like exactly what it is: their house with him gone. She knows that she will feel every sad day and every sad night and every sad argument seeping up from the upholstery, pouring down the walls, pooling at the bottom of every stupid coffee cup they own. If someone is leaving, it will have to be her. She needs to bust a move.

"No, *I'm* leaving," she says. "I hate it here."

As Brian stands by the door, not sure what to do next, she tears out of the living room and back to the bedroom as though a flag had dropped, the starting pistol fired. She begins to cry and cry and pack things. Anything. The wrong things thrown wrongly into the wrong bags. Uncapped deodorant among the underpants, a pillowcase mistaken for a shirt. She makes a grab for the clock on the bedside table and knocks it onto the floor. *Fuck you, clock.*

Margaret drops onto the bed, defeated. She reaches for Brian's pillow and lifts it to her face. She can smell his hair, his skin. She gathers the fabric of the pillowcase into her hands and breathes him in.

Then she gives her nose a good, hard blow.

Smoothing out the fabric, she returns the besmirched pillow to its spot on Brian's side of the bed and heads to the closet for another suitcase. There you go, Brian, she thinks, sleep tight.

Back in the hallway, Brian is listening to the rummaging and sniffling in the bedroom. He can't believe his luck – he has delivered his news without having to endure too much hysteria and he will not have to move out of the house. Who would have guessed? He returns his suitcase to the closet and opens the front door, closing it behind him as quietly as he can. He will come back when the coast is clear. There is something he needs to attend to anyway.

He needs to see a man about a horse.

If you know what I mean.

The button factory

MARGARET WORKS IN THE communications department of a large insurance company, checking documents. That is her job – checker. Naturally, this is not a real title. The job is called 'Senior Editor.' But she has no illusions: checking is her game.

Checking that each document looks just right and exactly the same as its many brothers and sisters, checking that all punctuation is correct, that all things make sense in their bland way. Checking margins and font sizes, dates and places and the spelling of names. The pamphlets, booklets and press releases she checks are intended to show the world the good work that is being done here at the Company. (Years ago, Margaret had begun to call it 'the button factory' inside her head and when speaking to select friends. She is not sure why, but it makes her laugh every time.) She is impressed by the fact that, after having read hundreds, maybe thousands of these documents over the past ten years, she has never come across anything that could possibly be interesting to anyone.

To be honest, insurance seems like the dumbest thing in the world to Margaret, like some kind of institutionalized gambling where the dealer almost always wins.

But hey, buttons aren't for everybody.

At the button factory, Margaret hates absolutely everyone. She hates everyone, every day, with a great big smile on her face. She especially hates people who are married, who have children, and who love their dogs. People who love their cats, their gerbils, their rats. Whatever. People and their boring lives. They talk and talk about nothing. It can be taxing, holding her work and co-workers in utter contempt for eight hours every day, but given the relatively generous size of the paycheque and the fact of her newly singled income, she thinks she can probably keep it going for several more years. The truth is that she doesn't mind the work that much: she is left alone to do orderly things that she finds oddly satisfying. And, frankly, she can't imagine what else she would do.

In her student days, she had had some grander idea of who she would be, studying philosophy (of all things), but it had been a very foggy kind of concept. If she is honest, she supposes that she had thought she would have some devastatingly interesting part-time job (Fashion designer! Television writer! Monkey trainer!) and a wealthy, charming husband who would manage the details of their lovely life. But, no. It was not her destiny. Margaret is only the checker and only at the button factory. And her husband, now in the arms of another, has only ever had limited wealth and diminishing charm.

Rabbit heart

DAY AFTER DAY MARGARET has arrived at her sad, little office at the button factory to spend the day checking and every evening she has gone home to her new small apartment. How unexpected, to be living alone in her own apartment at the age of thirty-five! She could not have predicted it.

The first weeks, strangely, had been splendid. After the cramped heat of living with someone so disgruntled, so utterly at odds with her, the apartment had felt expansive and cool. She breathed deeply, striding from room to room, making adjustments – fluffing up pillows, straightening pictures. Everything was new! New coffee and tea in new canisters on the kitchen counter, bright white sheets on her own bouncy bed, towels still bearing the creases from being folded and stacked in the store. Every evening she had let the sun go down without turning any lights on. She let darkness and quiet fall on the apartment. She would sit on the couch thinking nothing, being perfectly still. No music playing, no television blaring. Her breath was slow, her eyes closed. She was down in the pit with Yogi Satyamurti, after all.

Margaret had found giving up (partial) home ownership to be an enormous relief. She was no longer on high alert for dripping taps, the whiff of gas, unidentifiable ticking noises in the walls or pipes or vents. The sounds of a giant, unforeseen cash leak. She has given her home repairs over to a higher power: The Landlord.

Weekends, she has spent buying things that her ex, Brian, would have hated: a boxy, black couch for the living room, a massive, ornate, gold-framed mirror for the hallway. But the task that has given her the most pleasure has been seeking out and purchasing – at garage sales, flea markets, thrift stores – the ugliest and silliest decorative plates ever made and hanging them in a sort of gallery on her kitchen wall. There is one with the crew of Star Trek in their bright tunics, the Milky Way glittering in the black sky behind them; one with a dragon serving tea to a little boy in the woods.

Kittens playing chess, Jesus playing baseball and – her favourite – the Legends of Wrestling collector's plate. The neon-green plate features eight meaty, orange wrestlers in their trademark costumes (kilts, executioner's hoods, leopard-spotted underwear and so on), *holding hands*.

Glaring out from the plate, looking tough, holding hands with their pals.

It had seemed to Margaret that the place was coming together. Walls were painted, curtains were hung. She had found herself singing as she worked and loving the sound of her voice echoing through the apartment. She had thought that everything was just fine. Until one day.

One Saturday afternoon, she is surveying her living room, admiring the just-hung pictures, when she finds herself filled with pain and wonder, thinking of him. Brian. How happy they had been to find each other so many years ago. How perfectly sweet his face had seemed to her, how she had loved everything about him. She loved the shape of his fingernails and the hair on his arms and his soft, plump earlobes. Her small heart hurts. It is fluttering, racing like a tiny rabbit heart. She is squandering heart beats, leaking life-force as she bends slowly to the ground. She is on her knees and she presses her forehead into the carpet. She waits to throw up or to cry, but this will come later.

For now, she will stay here in this prayer position, quietly breathing, hoping to disappear.

How perfectly sweet his face

When Margaret met Brian, she believed in love, was burning with the possibility of it. Her experiences with dating had, to that point, been madly various. She had come face to face with the phantasmagoria of teenage-boy ardour: its clumsy fumbling, relentless goading, stinging cruelty; its infuriating shyness and pure, non-stop, fun-loving enthusiasm. And she was still game. She believed there were greater things ahead. She had left home for school convinced that she would know true love the minute she saw it and that it would be enchanting in a way that no other human could possibly understand. And it would not come from her home town.

In early adolescence Margaret had consumed mass quantities of girl-detective books, which invariably featured – along with the mystery – a chaste romance between the spunky heroine and some clever and polite boy. These romances unfailingly culminated with hand-holding and the presentation of a heart-shaped locket or an engraved bracelet and a tearful goodbye: summer camp or the ski vacation or the stay at the farm had ended. She had pictured these boys as kind of girly and big-eyed, with neat feathered hair in the style of Shaun Cassidy or Andy Gibb. A boy like that would smell like soap and be nice to your parents and giggle with you like one of your girlfriends. You would never feel nervous or embarrassed around a boy like that. She read *Teen Beat* magazine and cut out pictures and listened to records and dreamed of their existence.

Meanwhile, in the school yard, boys smelled like bananas and salami. They would chase girls until they fell over, rub snow in their faces, pinch them hard. This kind of thing could make Margaret cry with rage and press her legs together with excitement at the same time. It made her feel embarrassed and weak and spiteful. The thought of kissing a real boy made her feel sick to her stomach.

She would, as one might expect, overcome her aversion. Her tastes would turn from girl-detective books to trashy vampire stories,

from the Bay City Rollers to the Sex Pistols.
Boys would start to look and smell delicious.
Like men.

Margaret remembers the day – the very second – she fell in love with Brian. She had noticed him in several of her classes, noticed that in each one he had managed to secure the seat directly behind her. She had made a decision to sit in the very front row, determined to like university ten times more than she had liked high school and to show her professors that she was not afraid to be called upon, even when she had no idea what was going on and was likely to make a complete fool of herself. She was ready to be wrong and to learn. She was, to be honest, a bit cocky. No doubt, she was also a bit tiresome. But she was eager. In those first years away from home she walked around with the feeling that she was on the verge of every huge thing – of adult life, of understanding the world and herself in a new, earth-shattering way – and she felt certain that she was on the verge of discovering a great, lifelong love.

Margaret had noticed Brian but had not given him much serious thought. She knew his name, knew his style of question in class. (His questions were always pointed, but prefaced with what she felt were falsely modest disclaimers. "I could be wrong, but ..." or "Maybe I have misunderstood, but ...") She knew what he looked like. He was tall and skinny and messy, folded into the chair behind hers. There were holes in most of his clothing – his jeans, his shirts, his shoes and, as she would find out later, even his socks and underwear.

She knew he was a wiseass and she had decided to disregard him entirely.

On the day in question, she was already seated, waiting for the other students to get settled, for the professor to arrive, for the adventure to begin. Her cheek was resting on her palm, her elbow on her desk, when Brian reached forward, closed his hand around her wrist and turned her watch toward him to check the time. She could feel the skin tighten over her whole body and when she turned – half-affronted, half-wide-open with hope – to look at him, he smiled the most beautiful and suggestive smile. And that was the second she knew with a confidence never again repeated, that she was in love with Brian.

She took a moment to really look at him. His eyes were bright and blue and full of ridiculous ideas. He had the shadow of a beard on his jaw. Dark, possibly filthy hair rose in perfectly coiled springs from his head.

"What," she asked, "are you doing?" She had wanted to deliver this with some edge, some *hauteur*, but could not stop herself from grinning. Giggling like an idiot girl.

"Checking the time." This was whispered directly into her ear as the professor entered the room and class was launched. Her face burned red hot and she could hear a hum like mosquitoes in her ears. So there it was. The beginning of great love, exactly as she had expected it to be: immediately recognizable, far from home and hotter than Hades.

Hotter than Hades

MARGARET KNEW SOMETHING else about Brian. She knew that he had a girlfriend. He had a girlfriend who was the subject of much campus gossip and curiosity for one very good reason: she was not a girl at all, but a thirty-year-old woman who worked in a bank. To nineteen-year-old Margaret, this was like saying, "She is from Mars and is green," or more eerily, "She is old and has a boring job." The motive for this liaison for either Brian or this woman was completely unfathomable. It baffled the mind. Margaret would rather die than sleep with someone ten years her senior and she presumed that by the time she was thirty, she would have more sophisticated, if as yet unimagined interests than bedding students. Being young and on the side of true love, Margaret did not see this girlfriend as an obstacle, nor did she feel guilt for the romance she planned to embark upon or how it might feel for the silly old bank teller to be cast aside (as she surely would be). In her view, it was time for the woman to get a grip, to move along. Show's over.

Margaret also believed that the power of true love was not to be reasoned with, nor bound by the rules of polite society. True love was a steamrolling kind of thing, once engaged, and pity the fool that got in its way. She presumed that all people were likely to find themselves on the wrong side of it, at one point or another.

What did vex her was that Brian continued to see his *lady friend*, when he was so clearly in love with another (namely, Margaret). He followed Margaret around, in and out of classrooms, through corridors; he waited outside her dormitory, lurked in the nightclubs she frequented. They laughed and flirted and blushed bright red. And all the while he continued his occasional dates with Shelley the bank teller. This, Margaret found richly insulting. She resisted all advances. Her phone rang almost every evening (except when he was otherwise engaged) and every phone call went something like this:

"Yes?"

"Is your name really Margaret Atwood?"

"No."

"What's the *H* stand for?"

"None of your business."

"Come over."

"Not a chance."

"Please. 232 Oak Street. You know how to get here. It's so close!"

"No."

"Please."

"Where's your girlfriend?"

"At home, I suspect."

"Why don't you call her, tell her to go to hell and then call me back?"

Silence.

"Come over."

"I'm hanging up now."

"Come over!"

Margaret would put the phone down, tickled. She felt desired, pursued. And it was exhilarating to think that she might be luring him away from another woman. She felt like a seductress and a conspirator.

Until she started to feel like a loser.

Margaret began to smart from the humiliation of not being decisively chosen. After a few weeks of this lukewarm courtship she began to get testy. She started picking up the phone and upon determining that it was him, hanging up without a word. Then one day she found him woebegone on her front step.

"I told her".

"Who?" She looked at her nails.

"Shelley." His face stiffened slightly with irritation and embarrassment. "It wasn't easy."

"And what exactly did you tell this person?"

"I told her I couldn't see her anymore."

Margaret waited. She hadn't been asked a question as far as she could tell and she was not interested in hearing much more about Shelley.

"It's going to be OK now," he said.

"What is?"

"You and me!"

"Are we dating?" Here, finally, she began to smile. "Have I been asked for a date?"

They did not in fact go on a date, but went directly to her bed where they would spend an unbroken string of dozens of hot tangled-up nights.

In Margaret's small student bed, she and Brian will, as most lovers do, tell the stories of their lives so far. They will talk about movies and religion and music and politics and they will imagine – without success – what their lives will be like in ten years.

They will watch the sun come up and go down.

They will have sex relentlessly because they are young and happy and in love and their parents are far, far away. They will have sex while mostly asleep, while crying, when sick with the stomach flu, and when they are too sore and really should stop. They will kiss with terrible, unthinkable morning breath and it will all seem just right.

Fifteen years later, Margaret will scold herself for not being more wary of Brian's budding penchant for infidelity. Clearly he was rotten with the cheating impulse from Day One. She will wonder, too, if Brian's bank teller was also a cheater, supplementing a dull marriage with the occasional taste of delicious spring Brian lamb, such that he was. Yes, she will spend a great deal of time considering Brian's bank teller, how she had dismissed her out of hand as dull and outdated. Had she known anything at all, she might have been jealous; she might have fretted over whether she measured up. Probably this woman had shown Brian a thing or two. Probably, and she hated to think this, Margaret had benefitted from Brian's year-long, one-on-one training program with an older woman. Ugh.

And probably, the bank teller didn't really give a damn when Brian stopped visiting.

Worst of all, if she hadn't been such a mug, such a complete moron, Margaret might have suspected that Brian hadn't stopped visiting the bank teller at all.

But all of this scolding and thinking and suspecting and kicking of one's own ass would come later. On that day, the youngsters were coiled together and tucked tight into the steamroller single bed of their romance. Great storms lay ahead and petty ugly everyday things. But on that evening so long ago they were naked and hot and golden and smiling their stupid faces off.

Golden

IN THOSE HAPPY DAYS, those early days of their relationship, there were times when Margaret would lie flat on her back feeling amazingly heavy and listening to a sound deep in her head.

Maybe it was her blood streaming through her body, her heart pounding, her nerves singing like violin strings.

Sometimes if she could lie perfectly still for long enough the sound would take on several distinct strains, some high, some low. It groaned like a pipe organ.

Sometimes she even thought that she could hear words or chanting, a clicking kind of rhythm.

Sometimes if she closed her eyes she could imagine herself passing out of her body, levitating and glittering like a magician's assistant, the air around her like warm honey. Instead of falling asleep, she could rise up into it, shining like a new penny.

Up, up and away.

The penny

AFTER SEVERAL MONTHS and some coaxing, young Margaret would pack up her worldly possessions and move into Brian's apartment. He had cleared out his top three dresser drawers and two shelves in the medicine cabinet. He had stocked the kitchen with the everyday things she liked: pumpernickel bread and canned tuna; cream for coffee; blueberry yoghurt and grapefruits; granola, popcorn and even a few bags of fried pork rinds. He had changed the sheets and cleaned the toilet and he stood there grinning.

"Fit for a queen! An empress! For Margaret who loves pork rinds!" This was Brian: King of the Grand Gesture.

"Thank you." She could barely say it, she was so touched by his effort and so amazed that she was actually going to live in this place with him like a grown-up. It was like flying. "I love you."

"Hungry?" said Brian.

They would live there in his bachelor apartment for five full years, until they could afford a slightly bigger apartment and then they would marry. They would marry in an old-fashioned ceremony, white dress and all, with their friends and families looking on, moist-eyed and hopeful.

After graduating, Margaret had become what people were calling "underemployed": she worked as a waitress, part-time at the library, in record stores, in offices and finally she would land her button factory proofreading job where she remains, grumbling, to this day. Lucky for Brian, she was clever with money and her job paid reasonably well, as he would spend many more years in school while she bored herself to death at work every day, paying the tab.

Gradually, Brian transformed himself into a new, cleaner, more grown-up version of himself: Brian the lawyer, Brian the bigwig. His curly hair was cropped, his tattered student wardrobe replaced with increasingly expensive suits. Suddenly, he was always busy doing important work on important files and making important calls to important clients. And acting like he was in charge of the world.

She had created a monster. Or at least paid his way through law school.

Margaret and Brian would move to a bigger city and finally buy that house with the suitcase-harbouring front hall closet. Brian would wear his fancy suits and work late and travel all over the country and he would charm the pants off of every woman he met. Short ones, tall ones, fat ones, skinny ones. Margarets and Shelleys and Heathers and Lindas (and, for that matter, Jennifers and Katies and Tiffanys and Brittanys). Legions. Enough pants off enough women to circle the globe twice. It would take Margaret a long time to figure out why she should merit so many lavish presents and so little sex in those early years of her marriage.

But in the end, as they say, the penny dropped.

The raft

MARGARET HAS SIXTEEN NEW MESSAGES.

Sixteen. The light on the phone has been blinking at her for ten days. An evil red eye blinking all day, blinking all night. Against her better judgement, Margaret finally hunkers down at the kitchen table and punches the code into the phone. Six messages are from her mother and ten are from an assortment of friends, ranging from the genuinely concerned to the frankly meddlesome. She does not want to talk to any of them. She cannot stand the thought of repeating her sad story over and over again, until it becomes completely meaningless. And she dreads hearing what others will say in return.

She will hear (a) pity and (b) that no one is surprised.

This is too infuriating to ponder.

She is certain that everyone around her has been fully aware of Brian's exploits and that they have pitied her for years. Poor, sad fool! How horrible to be among the *pitied*, thinks Margaret. How did this happen? She pictures herself on a raft pushed out to sea, a raft piled high with The Pitied: the mentally challenged, the socially awkward, the physically disfigured and the wives of cheaters. If only there were such a raft, she would hop on gladly. Oh, for the peace of the Raft of the Pitied! Instead she will be plagued with those who wonder, with a hand on her forearm and in hushed tones, how she's *getting on.*

Oh, shame and pity! Oh, the shame of being pitied! How absolutely mundane, how boring her suffering seems, how utterly her own fault. If at least she had been the one to leave her no good husband, she might have been congratulated. She might have felt triumphant. Good for her! It was about time! But it was she who had been left. Discarded at last. Yesterday's girl, last year's model. A doormat of a mid-thirties nobody. And she feels stupid and trivial. There is real suffering in the world and she knows that hers is only a drop in the great sad ocean.

Margaret is thinking of an article she read in the paper the other day. (She has taken to reading the *New York Times* on Sundays in an attempt not only to fill the hours and distract herself from the empty, forward-reaching tunnel of her life, but also to become someone more connected to the happenings of the world, more *in the know*.) The article in question chronicles the lives of two elderly Brooklynites, Lillian and Julia.

The two were sisters, never married, who lived their simple lives together in the home they were raised in, the home their parents had left to them. They did office work and went bowling on Tuesdays, enjoying each other's company. They were heading steadily toward a quiet retirement when their seventeen-year-old nephew fled an abusive home to live with them. It went well for a long while, the article says, they lived as a family for many years.

Then the nephew had an accident, got hooked on painkillers. Then cocaine, then crack. He begins to bully them, to beat them if they don't give him money. They lose their house, their possessions. They are forced to beg on the streets. They are old ladies who sleep on the floor. They sleep in their clothes and coats in case their nephew wakes them up and sends them outside to beg for crack money. They have blackened eyes, are losing weight, have lost everything they ever worked for. They cry quietly together because they have lost their mother's china and they are ashamed. The newspaper tells Margaret that this is one of hundreds of cases in New York City alone, of "elder abuse." There have been sixteen murders this year in New York City of old people by their relatives.

She has also read in the *New York Times* that children are dying in Africa. This is something heard so frequently and for so many generations that it is hard to make it mean anything to the mind or the heart. But they are there and they are dying by the million, by the acre. They are dying of AIDS and starvation. They are dying of diarrhea because the water is dirty. (Margaret imagines, for a minute, *dying* of *diarrhea*.) They are fighting wars and begging in the streets and cooking meals for workers at coffee plantations and they are falling down dead by the million.

Twenty-six countries in Africa are among the twenty-seven countries with the world's highest child mortality rates. Because of the war in Congo 3.8 million people have died – half of them children under five. In Sierra Leone three out of ten children die before they are five.

And on and on.

Millions and millions, year after year.

And this is just the beginning of the suffering to be found in the newspaper on any given day. There is much more. Women are beaten to death in their own homes. Children are bought, sold, sodomized, killed. There are gangs and cartels and rings and more. People are despised and maligned, beaten and murdered because they are black or Jewish or gay or just plain wrong. Wars are tearing up the earth. The air, the water, the soil is poisoned.

It is not good news in the *New York Times*. Margaret does not understand how anyone lives, least of all her.

Not: how does anyone live through this or that?

Just: how does anyone *live*?

Why bother?

And anyone who looks like you

SIX MONTHS INTO HER SINGLE LIFE, Margaret is looking back at her marriage like a detective or a coroner: she has some questions and she wants some answers.

Generally, she wonders if almost all marriages are doomed to ruin of one kind or another. She has looked around and has found very few examples of success. She sees couples shattering or unravelling. Or just daily tending their gardens of petty grievances, steadily working their way up to full-blown hatred. Specifically, she wants to know why Brian cheated and why she, Margaret, put up with it for so very long. Neither thing on the surface makes much sense. Yet these two things together created the push-me/pull-you dynamic that was the basis of their marriage for ten years. Finally, and she is not quite ready to look this in the eye, she wants to know if she has it in her to ever believe in such a foolish thing as *love* again.

Margaret had always known that she never held Brian's full attention. He was an expansive flirt: women loved his company (men, less so). He was funny and charming, held doors open and carried bags, helped old ladies across the road. This good behaviour allowed him a lot of leeway. He was able to get away with things other men would never dare to attempt. She had loved his daring, was charmed by his charm. He was like a social rock star and in the beginning Margaret had loved him like a groupie. She had felt a kind of (pathetic, when she looks back on it) alpha-female victory at the end of any given evening out – no matter how many women had caught his eye or laughed at his jokes, she was the winner, the wife. She had felt a lot of silly pride in having landed such a catch.

Margaret has been trying to figure out exactly when she realized that Brian was unfaithful and she finds that a couple of moments bubble up from the timeline in an ugly way.

She remembers a certain evening when they had thrown a party. She can't remember exactly what the occasion had been. Possibly they had been celebrating some success of Brian's at work. In any event, the evening had been a great deal of fun, rooms packed with people, plenty of delicious food and lots to drink. Margaret had been pleased and relieved. Hosting parties always made her feel like a bit of an imposter – she felt like a teenager masquerading as a grown-up. There was always a moment when the house was clean, the food prepared, the bar stocked, when Margaret felt certain that no one would come, that it would all be ridiculous. It was always with a flood of relief and a touch of hysteria that she welcomed the first guests. On this specific occasion, Margaret had felt herself coasting toward the end of the evening feeling exhausted and as though everything had gone alright.

The party had abruptly come to an end, as parties sometimes do, with everyone suddenly realizing how tired they were and finding themselves unable to muster up the energy to start a new story or tell another joke. A silence had fallen and people began clearing their throats and saying what a good party it had been and making their way toward the exit. There had been a crush of people at the door and Margaret remembers chatting with a friend while watching Brian out of the corner of her eye. He was saying goodbye to a woman he worked with, a woman who was young and single and pretty. He kissed her on each cheek then looked around, mugging, as though checking to see if the coast was clear. The pretty girl laughed. Then he leaned in to kiss her cheek again and then slowly kissed her ear, her neck. His hand slid around her waist and he pulled her against him and then let her go abruptly, laughing. The girl stumbled away, waving awkwardly in Margaret's direction, and made her way out the door and into the night. Blushing and smiling with tears in her eyes, Margaret looked back to her friend and wished her a safe drive home. She turned her back on the scene and retreated to the kitchen where she started the long, mind-numbing process of cleaning up. This was, Margaret thinks, shortly before their first wedding anniversary.

She also remembers a night like many others when she lay awake in bed, fuming, waiting for Brian to come home. He had been out of town on business for several nights and had been due back at dinner time. She had cooked a meal. She had bathed and done her hair, put on creams and perfumes and lotions. She had put on a new outfit.

Then Brian had called to say that he had run into a colleague on the plane and that they were going to stop for a drink. He wouldn't be late. Margaret ate dinner alone, cleaned up the kitchen, put away the leftovers. At 11:00 p.m., she took off her nice clothes and put on her prettiest nightgown and tried hard not to be angry, hoping to salvage some kind of homecoming sweetness from the evening. At 2:00 a.m. she heard him come in and she pretended to be asleep. He crawled into bed stinking of booze and – Margaret had been shocked to find it so clearly identifiable – *vagina*.

This was the moment when Margaret stopped wanting to have sex. Ever. Her body turned cold; the shutters closed. They had been married for five years and would be married for five more.

Margaret thinks now that it was probably also around this time that she had stopped finding his jokes funny, that she started to watch his mouth while he ate. The grease on his lips, the sounds he made while he chewed made her want to vomit. She had begun to find that he smelled bad all the time, that his clothes hung off him in a ridiculous way. The list had grown as time went on: she hated the way he brushed his teeth and she hated finding his hair stuck to the soap; she hated the way he laughed with a vacant look in his eyes, the way he cleared his throat all the time; she hated his stupid boxer shorts and the chipper way he answered the phone. Etcetera. And so on. Every single fucking thing.

Yet she stayed. She stayed and the whole world became uglier and uglier to Margaret. Instead of leaving she undertook a series of silent protests: she stopped wearing silky nightgowns, reverting to giant t-shirts and big, unflattering, old underwear; she stopped wearing her wedding ring and stopped going to the hairdresser. She stopped wearing make-up or perfume and stopped 'watching her figure.'

Why had she stayed? Simple. Because the spell had worked. The process was complete. All of her power was gone. He was a winner and she was a loser. She could feel the giant *L* emblazoned on her forehead. She had no friends, but was scared to do things on her own.

This is what she had become. Sullen and helpless.

And, frankly, dowdy.

She stayed and silently wished, one thousand times per day, that he would fuck right off. Which is exactly what he did.

The middle of the night

IT IS THE MIDDLE OF THE NIGHT and Margaret can't sleep. She can't sleep and here is why: she has done a bad thing. Not just that: she has done a bad thing and she will pay. She will pay by agonizing in bed instead of sleeping, and she will pay at the office tomorrow. But we get ahead of ourselves. First, the bad thing. Or, rather: first, some background; second, the bad thing.

When Margaret was thirteen years old and reeling from disgust and irritation with her first period she started to notice crusty, itching patches of skin on the palms of her hands and on the tops of her feet. The patches were round, about the size of silver dollars. There was a centre of grey, peeling scales, surrounded by a brilliant, blood-red corona. They were hideous and, as previously mentioned, itchy. Unfortunately scratching didn't help. When Margaret scratched at them they burned, and then bled, then continued to itch. She ran tearfully to her mother who she suspected would be of no help at all.

Margaret's mother, a scattered and distracted woman who appeared to be only marginally interested in parenthood, applied a series of home-concocted poultices to Margaret's hands and feet over the next several weeks with worsening results. By the time a trip to the doctor was finally organized, Margaret's patches had doubled in size and become nicely septic. With one look the doctor proclaimed his diagnosis: psoriasis, with a heaping side of infection. They were hustled out the door with prescriptions for ointment and antibiotics. Margaret would continue to have recurring bouts of psoriasis in the same spots throughout her life. When the psoriasis was not active, it was never entirely gone; pinkish scars remained on her hands and feet, possibly as a result of that first painful and ill-managed experience.

Over the years she had begun thinking of her psoriasis as her 'stigmata' due to its peculiar locations. She and Brian (neither of them being very religious or very subtle in their humour) had

had many caustic laughs over this, especially when her flare-ups coincided with Easter or Christmas. He had thought her wry.

That is the background. Now, here is the bad thing.

On an ordinary weekday morning Margaret had entered her small office at the button factory to find Lenny, her supervisor, sitting in her chair, looking distinctly ill at ease. This was unprecedented. She had come to a dead stop, just short of landing (unthinkably) in his lap. He said, "I need to speak with you, Margaret. Come to my office." She had followed him, filled with dread and ready to receive some very bad news.

It seems that Margaret, in an awkward attempt at conversation around the photocopier, had made a crack about her aforementioned condition. She had made a joke, as should probably never be done, about the Crucifixion. She seems to recall receiving a sign of encouragement from one of her co-workers – a smirk or at the very least, a raised eyebrow. Tragically, she had gone further. She had mentioned that at Easter, she also had a stinging halo of pimples at her hairline and a stabbing pain in her side.

People had backed away politely, chuckling unconvincingly, murmuring excuses. Margaret had completed her photocopying and gone about her business, wondering only for a moment why she could never quite get the social things right, why she could hear her own voice when she was talking as though she were using a megaphone in an empty gymnasium. Where *was* that laugh track anyway?

If only that had been the worst of it. Apparently there had been, among her audience around the photocopier, a young and earnest Christian woman named Marie. Marie had only just started working at the button factory and Margaret remembers being introduced to her by Lenny on her first day. She had been struck by her obvious youth. Everything about her seemed so clean and bright, so smooth and new.

Marie was bubbly and friendly and twenty years old. She made Margaret feel like a burlap sack filled with porridge.

Marie had not found the joke about stigmata wry. She had

found it hateful and embarrassing and, in the end, had registered a complaint with Lenny. And so Margaret, seated in his office, has had to endure the recounting of her pathetic and inappropriate performance by her smug supervisor. She knows, too, that throughout the day she will also have to endure the averted gazes of her co-workers and wonder how much they know about the complaint and her talking-to and what they are thinking. She will be forced to contemplate what, perhaps, they have always thought about her. Finally, Lenny has informed her, she will have to endure a full-day workshop entitled, Working Together: Difference in the Workplace.

Margaret sits as straight as she can in the itchy chair across from her boss, who is staring angrily at the blotter on his desk. Her diaphragm is trembling, the weep machine threatening to bubble into gear. She steadies herself and is about to get up to leave when Lenny clears his throat. He starts to talk or mutter, shaking his head. She had hoped he had finished with her, but settles back into the naughty chair and stares out the window at the sky above his head.

"Margaret, Margaret, Margaret."

"I know."

"Margaret, Jesus!"

"Oh my God. I know. I *know*."

"What are you doing to me? Why?"

"I don't know."

"Is there something wrong with you? I mean, what makes a person say things like that? Is it so hard to just not say things?"

"I was wrong. There's probably something wrong with me. You're right. I can stop talking at work. I don't need to talk." She is trying to think of something to say that will make him want to keep her in this stupid, stupid job that is the only thing on the plus side of the balance sheet of her pitiful life. Inspiration is not forthcoming. Better to leave it there. She waits.

Lenny is rubbing his eyes with the palms of his hands. He rubs too hard. He rubs until, when he finally opens his eyes and looks at her, he can only see a black blob with blue quivering around the edges. He likes her better that way anyway.

Lenny sighs. He shakes his head slowly. Margaret notices that his normally brown, flat hair seems fuzzier than usual, that parts of it look patchy and yellow. Has he done something to it? He doesn't look quite right.

"I have my own problems, you know. I have work to do. I have a family. And every time I turn around there is someone on this floor acting like an idiot for no reason. There is a mess and then I have to fix it. Do you think I enjoy this part of my job, Margaret?" Or any other part of it, he is thinking.

"No."

"Alright, then."

"Alright."

"OK. Back to work. Quietly, please."

"As a mouse. I swear."

And now here is Margaret, wide awake in the middle of the night. She has replayed the scene at the photocopier, as well as the scene in Lenny's office, over and over and over again in her head. Play, pause, rewind, play. There is a blue light from the street flooding her bedroom and she is lying in her bed on her side, crying. The tears run from one eye, over the bridge of her nose and into the other eye. They run from this second, bottom eye directly onto the pillow, which is already soaked and cold.

She is not making any noise.

She is not trying to stop herself from crying or to wipe the tears away.

She is just quietly soaking her pillow and wishing as hard as anyone can wish for anything, for sleep or peace. It is this powerful wishing that brings it on; this is the moment when the aliens make their first visit to wretched Margaret Atwood.

The aliens

THAT'S RIGHT: ALIENS. Although this first incident was not much of a visit. It was more of a checking-in, a how-do-you-do, a testing of the waters. The aliens have been watching Margaret for months now and they are interested in her progress. Before tonight, they have watched from far away, using a device that has no name that earthlings could possibly understand, but that transmits images from her apartment to their ship. Think of it as a television screen, only much, much better.

For all this time the aliens have been biding their time in their ship, hovering high above the city, above the clouds, hanging suspended in the dark with the stars. They have seen Margaret pace around, placing objects here and there. For months they have watched and they have seen the same things almost every day: they have seen her wake up, shower, get dressed and leave for work; they have seen her come home, make dinner, brush her teeth, and go to bed. They have seen this boring clockwork routine play itself out over and over again in the lit box of her small apartment in this crazy cluster of human dwellings and machinery.

They have seen other things, too. They have seen Margaret's every sad, shameful, private moment. For example, they were watching that Saturday afternoon when Margaret fell to her knees and placed her forehead on the floor. They have seen it all: urinating, defecating, nose picking, even (and only once) masturbating. It is the crying that upsets them, though. This and the complete lack of visitors.

On the night of the first visit, several giddy aliens are clustered around the screen on the ship as the Leader teleports to Margaret's apartment. He is practically invisible! He emits a soft, blue-green glow as he descends, brushing the treetops, and settling on Margaret's bedroom windowsill. He crouches there for a moment, resting.

Back in the ship, the aliens consider Margaret, lying in her bed.

They like her silky, brown hair and the way it spreads out on the pillow. They like her plump cheeks and the delightful girlishness of her face. They like the way her body curves so sharply inward in the middle, the way the sheets follow the line of her body. And their green, alien hearts lift as they recognize the blue glow of their leader shining in through the window onto her face.

The Leader moves quietly across the room to Margaret's bed. He stands there, waiting for her to notice him and, no surprise, she does. Margaret rolls very quickly from her side onto her back and sits upright, back pressed against the headboard, staring. The Leader stays as still as he can (though it is difficult – he finds these visits to humans so *exciting*!). Margaret's heart is pounding. She contemplates reaching for her glasses but is afraid that this will provoke some kind of violent reaction from the creature that confronts her. She tries to get a good look anyway. (To do this without glasses, she must close one eye tight and really squint with the other.)

The alien waits.

Margaret H. Atwood is strangely moved by what she sees – it is an alien, fully recognizable from television, the movies, books. He is green, of course, and big-headed. His eyes are black almonds and his arms unreasonably long. All of this fits the standard profile. What surprises her is how beautiful he is – he stands straight and tall and stares directly into her eyes. His skin is not entirely green, but a shimmering green and blue and gold. It reminds her of shot silk. Probably she is exaggerating or getting this wrong, but it also makes her think of the wet skin of dolphins. What unnerves her (and what no amount of daytime television could have prepared her for) is that he is completely nude and has a very human-looking penis. But she tries not to focus on this.

The Leader leans down and places a hand on Margaret's forehead and runs it gently down over her face and rests it on her chest. She feels the heat and weight of it. He brings his face up close to hers and says, as so many aliens have said to so many humans before, "You will not remember this." Sadly, he reflects upon how unevenly this technique has worked on humans in the past – witness the proliferation of abductee accounts.

But it works this time on Margaret.

She will sleep soundly until morning and she will not remember a thing.

Two

Werewolves

THE NEXT MORNING MARGARET scrambles out of bed to get ready for work and for a few glorious minutes she has forgotten all about her talk with Lenny, all about the sad state of affairs her work life has become. Then gradually it settles darkly on her shoulders and she hangs her head low. She showers, eats her breakfast, brushes her teeth. She feels numb, hollowed out. She tries on no less than six unsuitable outfits. Finally, she settles on what she thinks must be the most blameless combination possible – black pants, cream shirt, the tiniest of gold earrings – and bolts for the door, praying that she is not too late to catch the bus.

Oh, how Margaret despises the bus and all it stands for! She waits seething at the bus stop, checking her watch each minute, getting more and more agitated. She knows the busses never come on time but knowing doesn't help. Finally, the bus comes creaking and snorting to a stop, its door opening ten feet beyond the bus stop and Margaret and her fellow passengers grumble and bump and nudge and shuffle their way onboard. Some, the aliens notice, glance wistfully over their shoulders, wishing they could think of an excuse to turn around, to walk away from the bus and just stroll through the park on this fine, bright, crisp autumn day. The air, even in the city, even at rush hour, smells like leaves and apples and woodsmoke. The sky is as brilliant as chrome; the sun floods the street.

Once on the bus Margaret shrewdly surveys her options for seatmates, seeking someone who does not seem crazy, is not too large, is not likely to smell bad (this, she finds surprisingly hard to tell from just looking at people), and is not in the mood to *talk*. She settles on a slight teenage girl that is staring sullenly and fixedly out the window. Perfect.

Margaret takes her place and jams the buds of her earphones firmly into place. She likes to think of the music as a force field, preventing interaction with other humans. She has been wearing headphones and listening to music virtually every day since her early teens. She had saved her babysitting money for a full year in order to purchase her first giant cassette-tape-playing Walkman and it had been worth every penny. She remembers clearly the wonder of walking the streets for the first time with the soundtrack of her favourite music being piped directly into her ears. How much better the world seemed that way! It had made her feel like the star of her own private movie. She had also noticed that if the music was loud and she resisted catching anyone's direct gaze, her daily human contact was reduced significantly. Mission accomplished! Blessed technology, she thought, thank you for saving me.

For this morning's bus ride, Margaret has selected Warren Zevon, *Excitable Boy*, 1978. She has no idea why this music from so long ago, this voice now dead, is so appealing to her. In particular, she loves the idea of smartly dressed werewolves marauding through the streets of London. Eating beef chow mein and drinking pina coladas, ripping out lungs and mutilating old ladies. She wishes they would come to her office some time.

In spite of the music, Margaret can feel the body heat of the girl beside her. She swallows thickly, smelling the mix of perfume and coffee breath and something like cottage cheese coming off her seatmate. She returns her focus to the werewolves. Those beautiful, seductive predators. Predators like Brian. Like that crack-bastard nephew of those old ladies in Brooklyn. Margaret ponders this for a moment: her sad self and the sad old ladies and their stupid, misspent love; the surprising derailment of their lives. She thinks about how everyone probably wants to be a werewolf or a crocodile or a lion, and how so many of us are feckless, blank-eyed wildebeests at heart.

Margaret straightens up and tries to create a millimetre of space between her and the stinking teenager who turns and glares for a moment, then turns back to the window. Warren sings the sad and triumphant story of Roland the Headless Thompson Gunner. Margaret glares back at the girl and imagines that revenge is sweet, even for the headless.

A lifetime later, the bus shudders to a stop in front of the good old button factory. Margaret rises on unsteady legs and clatters down the aisle and out the door with the rest of the herd.

The trampoline

MARGARET WALKS TOWARD HER office building in the same way she always does: as if she were fitted to a track. She has often had the impression that she could fall sound asleep – or be struck unconscious by a sharp blow to the head – and she would continue gliding toward and through the front doors of the building, onto the elevator and off again, veering toward her office and into her chair. Like a horrible proofreading zombie. She does not wave to anyone or say good morning though she passes many familiar faces along the way. This is nothing new: she hates everyone and most who know her take care to avoid her gaze. That's just the kind of gal she is!

Though today as Margaret walks past reception toward her desk, she can hear the quiet that only slightly precedes her. Anyone who has ever been a child in a schoolyard is familiar with the phenomenon: the way that the silence following vicious gossip has a certain strange and recognizable ring to it when compared to the silence that falls of its own accord, when nobody has anything left to say. Margaret tries not to take this personally, tries to believe she is imagining the tension in the air, but as she sits down at her desk she can feel the hair on the back of her neck standing up. She feels something rattle through her stomach.

Margaret's desk is perfect, or at least it is exactly the way she likes it: the L-shaped surface is clean and clear, except for three stacks of file folders. 'Stacks' is probably not the right word. The files are in three rows, fanned, with their labels showing. Each file folder contains a document to be proofread, along with any necessary reference material. This material might include related reports, glossaries, similar documents produced in the past, etc. The rows represent, from left to right, the following categories: New, Reviewed, In Progress. The 'new' files have not yet been examined, someone has just dropped them into her in-basket. The 'reviewed' documents have been given a once-over and Margaret has determined how long each document will take her to finish and what degree of priority she should place upon it. These are accompanied by tidy, detailed notes. Finally, those 'in progress' are just that. Once files are completed, they do not languish on Margaret's desk, but go directly to Lenny. She also keeps a running list on her computer, tracking which files are in which category at any given moment. This is her system and she never deviates from it. The excitement might kill her.

You will not find coffee mugs and cookie crumbs on Margaret's desk, certainly no apple cores or half-eaten sandwiches. The desk, she feels, is not a place for eating. Margaret despises receiving documents that have smudges on their corners or wrinkled coffee stains. She judges the people who produce these documents harshly. She views their actions as a personal insult. In her view, a person might as well have wiped his (or her) ass with the document and dropped it in her in-basket. There you go, Margaret! Over to you!

Disturbing the order of Margaret's desk this morning are two things: a large manila envelope sitting on top of her 'In Progress' files and the flashing message light on her phone. These things must be addressed before Margaret can begin her work for the day with a clear mind. With trepidation, she picks up the phone and keys in her code. The female message-service voice gives her the usual mechanical lowdown: "You have – *two!* – new messages. To listen to your messages, press *one!*"

Margaret cringes as she presses the button. She was hoping for only one message, preferably a wrong-number culprit hanging up just a moment too late. But there are two messages and both are bad. The first is from Lenny's assistant, Nancy. She wishes to confirm that Margaret has received the information package on her upcoming 'Diversity in the Workplace' workshop. Presumably, this is the offending brown envelope lying askew on Margaret's desk. Her face burns with fresh shame as she listens to the cheerful, business-as-usual delivery of the message, strongly suspecting that Nancy has told everyone who will listen all about Margaret's bad behaviour. Nancy has, no doubt, embellished the tale to make it even more delicious. No doubt, new lurid details have proliferated as the story has blown like a tumbleweed through the office. Margaret suspects that in the current version, she is standing completely nude at the photocopier, demanding that people examine her psoriasis and proclaiming herself the saviour.

The second message is from Margaret's mother, whose words are kind and whose tone is distinctly peeved. She would like to know how Margaret is doing, if she is still living at the same address and if she still has the same telephone number. It just seems as though she is never in. She is contemplating a visit to check on her, to make sure everything is alright. Margaret refuses to entertain this idea today. She knows that her mother is likely bluffing about the visit. She lives two thousand miles away and rarely manages to comb her hair; the idea that she could book an airplane ticket and pack a suitcase seems far-fetched, to say the least.

Margaret remembers when she started to scorn her mother, while still loving her, the moment when she realized that, although they were part of the same genetic chain and lived in the same household, they would never understand anything about each other. And generally speaking, it would be best if they just kept their views to themselves. Margaret was twelve years old and had been reading – and not fully understanding – a book about Einstein and his general theory of relativity. She loved the idea that space and time could be linked in a kind of fabric that could be wrinkled and bent and indented by matter. She was struck by a passage she had read that described the earth orbiting the sun the way a marble would circle a bowling ball placed in the centre of a trampoline. She had started to try to picture the space-time fabric around her in her everyday life and after a time, she felt she could see the waves made by her movement, that she could see the air wrinkling and waving around cars driving past her house. When she was falling asleep at night she thought she could feel the universe expanding, pulling away from her own body. She began to draw diagrams and keep notes.

Feeling she might be on the verge of some momentous discovery,

Margaret confided in her mother about her ability to see the fabric of space and time. Margaret's mother, whose name was and is Rose, stopped in the middle of lining her eyes with the maroon pencil she favoured. Margaret remembers it now as a clear snapshot: her mother sitting in her loud dressing gown, surrounded by filthy jars and brushes and half-squeezed tubes, the floor of her bedroom a sea of underpants and tissues. Margaret's mother rose up and placed her hands on little Margaret's skinny shoulders and looked into her face. Rose had only completed the making up of one eye and looked completely cockeyed and insane. She said, "Honey, stop. You're not making sense. Why don't you go outside for a while? It's beautiful out there."

Margaret already knew how beautiful it was out there. She had been outside all morning, waving her arms through the rippling fabric of the universe, for Christ's sake.

Now the aliens know, as does Margaret, that it was not a matter of Margaret being especially clever and her mother being especially dull. Both of them, in the aliens' estimation, were undeniably average humans in most ways. They believe that what divides them is one's talent for focus and the other's for distraction.

Back at the office, tucked into another wrinkle in the fabric, Margaret erases both messages and hangs up, slips the brown envelope into her bag, straightens up and gets on with her work.

Only 450 minutes to go!

The stall of shame

Mid-afternoon at the button factory and Margaret is uncharacteristically struggling to focus on the task at hand: she has been asked to edit the copy for a wheedling brochure designed to entice senior citizens to buy insurance. It brings to mind a recent article in the business section of the *New York Times* entitled, "Who's Preying on Your Grandparents?" The article described a scam performed by several large insurance companies (and a well-deserved class action suit against said companies) that went something like this: old people are offered free lunch and a seminar on safe investment strategies. At the lunch, they are asked to fill out surveys requesting detailed information about their assets and financial holdings. A few days later, they are visited by a salesman that offers them an investment with an immediate cash bonus and a good rate of return. The salesman leaves behind a pamphlet that explains, undoubtedly in the smallest of small print, that the annuity cannot be cashed without an outrageous penalty for fifteen years. In the likely event that the purchaser dies before the investment matures, his or her beneficiary will be required to pay an outrageous 'surrender fee' in order to access the funds.

Margaret has added this scheme to her list of why she is right about the shittiness of the world and all those who inhabit it. She tries to turn her attention back to the pamphlet and reluctantly plays her part in the sad charade. Stupid *New York Times*! It ruins everything.

As she works through the text, crossing out words and making notes in the margins, Margaret feels a sickening twinge at the bottom of her stomach and a sharp pain between her shoulder blades. A small beast burns a churning path through her guts. She denies. She blocks. She struggles to continue proofreading but Margaret realizes that her will is no match for the storm that is brewing.

She gets up from her desk wondering briefly if she has time to go to a bathroom on another floor of the building. Impossible. She heads directly to the ladies' room, hurtles herself into the first stall. Pulls down her pants, sits down heavily and lets fly a blistering stream of shit. Sweating, she rests her clammy forehead on her bare knees. She notes with relief that there is no one else in the bathroom. She may get away with it. A few tense seconds pass and she prays (really prays with words directed to God the Father) that the horrible episode is over. But, as all the world knows, diarrhea has no mercy. A shock of pain makes Margaret sit up sharply and she endures another noisy, burning, unstoppable storm. The stink is monumental. Margaret (you saw this coming) freezes as she hears the door of the bathroom open.

Marie and her friend Frances enter the bathroom and stop talking abruptly. They have hit a wall of *smell*. Margaret squints through the crack in the door. Of course it had to be Marie, her honey-haired accuser. Margaret resolves to bide her time. She sits tight as the young women regain their composure and set about their business. Stall doors are opened, delicate tinkling noises are made. The ladies snap snaps and zip zippers. They flush and exit the stalls. Hands are washed, lipstick applied, handbags are snatched up and high heels click across the tiles and out the door. *Hallelujah*. Margaret scrambles to pull herself together and get the hell out before someone else arrives. Mercifully, no one does.

Margaret feels she has won a small victory. A small, reeking victory. She emerges shakily from the bathroom and into the hallway to find (and maybe you saw this coming, too) Marie chatting with Lenny. They stop, acknowledge her with a nod and look away. Pale Margaret tries for a smile and settles for a grimace.

Never has a human felt so debased. She feels like walking shit. She lets her chin hit her chest as she makes her slow way back to her desk.

A hater, not a lover

THAT EVENING, MARGARET ENTERS her apartment fuming. She has been thinking hateful thoughts about Lenny and Marie and her mother for the whole miserable bus ride home. She slams the door so hard that the dishes rattle in the cupboards. However, the door, which is ill-fitted to its frame, hits the jamb and rebounds toward her at a terrifying pace. Margaret slams the door over and over again, each time more frantic than the last, begins to cry and curse and then closes it in the usual and only effective manner: by pulling upward on the knob with both hands and shoving her full weight against it with her hip.

Margaret notes with resignation that the message light on her phone is flashing. It is her mother, no doubt. Much to the aliens' dismay, she pours herself a bowl of cereal for dinner and ponders the tactical errors she has made in her relationship with her mother. As a young adult, Margaret had determined that the best way to avoid warring with her mother was to maintain a chipper, superficial relationship. She had achieved this, generally, by doing a lot of listening and encouraging and mindfully keeping all information about her own life to herself. Unfortunately, a couple of months ago, Margaret had made the misguided decision to talk to her mother – for the first time in her life – about sex. Now, predictably, everything is ruined. Her mother fancies herself a *confidante* and is eager to continue the conversation. Margaret, on the other hand, had realized her error immediately and has been wishing she could go back in time to correct it ever since.

Months of solitude had led Margaret, unwillingly, into a great deal of self-examination and as she watched the millionth television show reminding her that other people in the world were having (and mostly enjoying) sex, she got to wondering. There were shows about the sex lives of single women in New York, there were documentaries about sex among the over-fifty set, sitcom parents sneaking away to – har, har – have sex, and on and on. It seemed there were no shows about women in their mid-thirties who eat cereal for dinner and feel dead between their legs.

Margaret had begun to get the impression that there might be something wrong with her health or her mind. She understood why she had not wanted to have sex with her husband at the end of their marriage: she had hated him. That was simple enough. But now that he was gone there was still nothing. She did not desire men. Or women, for that matter. She did not crave sex no matter how many lonely months rolled by. She could not even conjure the remotest glimmer of arousal. Worried, Margaret had tested herself just to make sure: she had looked at men on the street and imagined them nude; she watched marginally dirty (foreign) movies and read marginally dirty (foreign) books.

Night after night, she would give it the old college try. Lying naked in her bed, she felt like a corpse on a slab. She tried to conjure a leading man – a movie star, a rock star, a high school crush from way back in the mists of time – but nobody ever seemed right. If she could focus long enough to make a selection, her mind created distractions, made excuses. She might remember that he was married, might notice a hairy mole on his neck. She fidgeted, her back itched, she was certain that she had to go to the bathroom.

Something was broken.

Even in her fantasies, she did not want to touch people or see their naked bodies. She would rather not. No thanks, I'm full.

The truth was Margaret had become a hater, not a lover. She had developed a wrenching disgust with the visceral reality of humans: she did not like to think of their mouths or their body hair or their various smells. She felt sick to her stomach if she looked too long at a person's scalp, the way it could be so pale and scaly. She did not like people's breath or their sweat. It goes without saying that she could not bear to think of people's genitals, or anything they might do with them. Margaret felt that she had somehow reverted back to a time in childhood when kissing and sex were *totally gross* and seemed completely incompatible with anything nice.

After having wrong-headedly convinced herself that this complete lack of libido could be an indicator of early menopause or possibly some form of cancer (of the brain? of the ovaries?), she had begun to panic. The more Margaret tried to stop thinking this way, the more panicky she became. She pondered going to the doctor but she knew, however, that this would involve a humiliating conversation followed by some humiliating examinations. And she knew that likely nothing was wrong with her at all; that she was likely to make a complete fool of herself. Finally she thought (and God knows why) that maybe her mother could shed some light on the situation. This was where the trouble began.

"Mom?"

"Margaret!"

"Can I ask you something?"

"Anything."

"Do you think there is a time in a person's life when you naturally go off sex altogether?"

"What are you talking about? What time in a person's life?"

"I don't know. Later in life. Or throughout your life. Do you think that things just slowly wind down? Is there some kind of hormone drop or something?" Margaret can't quite believe she has said this: 'hormone drop.' What the hell was that supposed to mean?

"Margaret. I think a person can probably be interested in sex for their whole life. If they are physically able and they have someone to have sex with. I mean there are certainly times when I feel less sexy than others, but I can usually be convinced, if you know what I mean. *Ha!*"

Cringing, Margaret is visited by the image of her father – his silence, his pale transparency. His frequent quiet retreats to the shed, to the basement, to the pharmacy where he had worked day after day, for so many years. Margaret's father had an air of Bob Newhart about him: defeated, wry and kind. He and Margaret had shared many knowing glances over the years at her mother's expense. But Rose had blundered on through the years, gaining power, as her father and his cardigans seemed to just fade into the background. Margaret can imagine him slowly taking on the muted colours of his environment, camouflaged against the fading wallpaper of the living room.

It was difficult to imagine her father 'convincing' her mother of anything. But sex! This was deeply disturbing.

Ignoring good sense, Margaret had decided to press on:

"Mom, I am not asking about your personal experience. I guess what I meant is: is there some kind of sexual decline that physically happens to women after a certain age?" Everything Margaret says sounds ludicrous now and she half-considers just pulling the receiver away from her ear and hanging up. She swallows a hard lump in her throat. It seems she is filled with tears these days, brimming with tears, ready to slosh over the top with the slightest bump or sway.

"Margaret, for Christ's sake. You're thirty-five years old. You are in your prime. You don't want to have sex because your husband was a bastard and because you are tired and sad and lonely. You know what? I would like to come see you. There are good deals on flights right now. Why don't you book some time off work and we can do something together, go somewhere. What do you think?"

Margaret is silent for a second. She thinks hard about what she could possibly say to dissuade her mother from coming. "Mom, I have to go now. Someone's at the door. I'll call you later." And she hits the magical hang-up button on the phone. The button that makes her mother disappear.

This is how the conversation had ended, with Margaret knowing full well that she would not keep her promise of calling back and Rose knowing with absolute certainty that the only thing for her to do was to make arrangements to visit her daughter as soon as possible.

Get me my medicine!

Having finished her cereal, Margaret pours herself half a coffee cup of gin. She knows there is something wrong with drinking gin by herself, straight, and from a coffee cup, but she is not sure exactly what it might be. She recalls once, when she was a teenager, she had been visiting a friend whose mother had felt moved – no doubt by some silly drunken stunt enacted by the two girls – to instruct them in the warning signs of impending alcoholism. The only one that Margaret could remember with any certainty was 'drinking alone,' of which she was certainly guilty. She was also guilty of going to different liquor stores each week so that the cashiers would not notice the frequency and uniformity of her purchases. Probably this was another bad sign.

On one such excursion, a young flower of a liquor store cashier had looked closely at Margaret's credit card, stopped dead, stared into her eyes and demanded to know if she was really Margaret Atwood, the famous Margaret Atwood.

Now this truly gave Margaret pause.

Over the years she had been subjected to many a wisecrack and many a sidelong glance on account of her famous name but not once had anyone been fool enough to actually mistake her for the woman herself. She considered her options. She wanted to say: "No. Margaret Atwood was born in 1939, the same year as my mother. Margaret Atwood has written no less than fifty books and presumably has vastly more important things to do than buy yet another bottle of gin from geniuses like you." She wanted to say: "Yes, I am Margaret Atwood. I am the glorious, world-famous, extra-clever, Canadian icon. Can I have my gin for free?" But what she really said was: "No, that's my mother. Margaret Atwood is my mother."

To tell the truth, though, none of these things – the coffee cup, the solitary imbibing, the rotating stores – seems to Margaret to be as disturbing as the sheer joylessness of her drinking. It is like taking medicine. Quick! Get me my medicine! Surely, this was a sign of something being badly askew in her life.

Nonetheless, Margaret takes her medicine and stares at the phone. The choices lie before her thus: check the phone message, likely from her mother and likely to send her into hours of guilt-baked bad thoughts; read the information package about her upcoming course on being nicer to people; or, drink more gin and watch some sad-assed television show. Frankly, the night is young and she can do all three things if she chooses, preferably in the order previously stated: guilt, fury, numbness, bed. She reaches for the phone. (The aliens watch and wait. They know what is coming.)

Checking her messages and preparing to hear the slightly loopy, sweet, irritating voice of her mother, this is what comes out of the phone:

"Margaret. This is Brian. You need to call me so we can sort some things out."

Margaret bristles. She hates the sound of his voice. It forces her to think about the face it comes out of.

Brian's game face

BRIAN LOVES TELLING PEOPLE what they need to do! And he loves to win. Winning is great! At sports, in his job, at a customer service desk in a department store, Brian loves to win! Sometimes he makes complaints even when he is happy, just to see if he can get something for free – a meal, an upgrade to first class, a voucher of some kind. Because even more than winning, Brian likes to get away with things. This is the engine that drives him. Brian remembers when he became conscious of it, when he first realized how much could be gained simply by having the nerve to ask a question.

Once, when Brian was a student, he had found himself at the back of a block-long line-up at the Registrar's Office. The line filled hallways, spilled down staircases, poured out the door and across the sunlit courtyard. He knew that the longer he waited the more likely it was that the courses he wanted to take would be full. He walked the length of the line and noticed a mousy, mildly pretty girl staring at the polished floor. She was about twelve people back from the front of the line; in Brian's estimation, there were about two hundred people behind her. He approached the girl. With a huge, goofy smile on his face, he said, "Let me go in front of you." The girl laughed at him and squealed, "No!" and the game was on.

"Please let me go in front of you."

"Why should I?"

"I was here first."

"No you weren't!" She was blushing now and Brian knew he was in.

"It will give us a chance to talk – we never talk anymore."

"I don't even know you!"

After a lot of giggling and a little bit more flirting Brian was firmly ensconced ahead of the girl. At this point, he determined never to remain at the back of any line, at least not without trying somehow to weasel his way forward. Not only might he save a lot of time, he would be thoroughly entertained.

Over time Brian became so good at this game that he began to set parameters to make it more challenging. He was not allowed to approach girls, only men. He would only target people in the front sixth of any line. At least once in a while, he had to attempt the person who was second in line (virtually impossible to convince). Finally, he was not allowed to offer any justification for his desire to take the place in front of the person. He could not say, "I will miss my train," or even, "This is an emergency." He was required to attain his place on the strength of his charm alone, never through sympathy. And he had to tell the truth: "Let me go ahead of you. Because I want to and because it won't make that much difference to you."

It was stunning how often it worked.

What now?

An hour later, Margaret is still staring narrow-eyed at the phone, empty coffee cup dangling from her thumb. What could he possibly want from her?

She had walked away from everything: the house, the car, the whole fuming, stinking mess. She had not asked for money or even for an apology (and it seemed to her that one or two – or three or four – were richly deserved).

She is aware that she must phone him back as soon as possible, that she needs to get it over with. Otherwise she will be consumed with anxiety. She will concoct absurd and ever-worsening scenarios in her mind. It will begin with the possible and distasteful – Brian and Sandie would like to have dinner together to talk things over; they think it is time that they all got to know each other a little better – and it will mushroom into the preposterous: Brian has taken an interest in exotic pets and wonders if Margaret would mind caring for his iguana while he and Sandie are in the Bahamas. Brian wonders if she could go on fertility drugs and donate some of her ova so that he and Sandie can start a family. He is taking a trip around the world and wonders if Margaret could carry him on her back, please.

Margaret picks up the phone and dials.

Her heart is sour and ugly.

Brian and Sandie are not in at the moment and this is the message that Margaret regrets leaving the second the words start sliding out of her mouth: "Hello, Brian. This is Margaret. I can't imagine what you could possibly want from me, but once your list is finalized, give me a call at your convenience. And go to hell. Thanks!" All of this delivered in the chipper, can-I-help-you voice of a teenage shopgirl. Perhaps she slurs her words just a little bit. Margaret places the phone back in the cradle and draws her hand back, as if the receiver were coated in something poisonous, something fool-making. No more phone calls tonight.

Deciding to forgo the information package from work, Margaret refills her coffee cup and heads for bed with the orange setting sun still shining in through the windows of her apartment. She locates the remote control, shucks and steps out of her clothes, which she leaves tangled on the floor, and gets into bed. She sits, propped up by two pillows, cup balanced on her chest, eyes glazed, for several hours. She cycles through the channels at increasing speed: sitcom, golfing, game show, unsolved mysteries; cop show, coroner show, news; cooking show, dating show, Japanese cartoons, music videos, more news. Power off. She fumbles the remote and the coffee cup onto her bedside table, knocking her alarm clock to the ground. She turns off the lamp and in the course of doing so knocks the remote and the cup off the table, as well. She curses, grunts, and then sleeps.

Meanwhile, high in the night sky, the aliens are preparing their Leader for another visit. In their glowing, hovering ship they fuss around him like excited bridesmaids – they pinch and tuck and pat and smooth. They stand back and assess. The Leader takes a deep breath and peers closely at the screen, looks at Margaret lying there, sleeping. She sleeps on her back, twisted in the sheet. From this angle, it looks as though she might be levitating, as if her body has lifted just slightly above the surface of the bed. Her hair radiates from her head and her mouth hangs open. Her eyes twitch and occasionally her brow furrows like a human baby's does when about to cry, and then it softens again. This will surely not be news to anyone, but the truth is that the Leader is quite taken with Margaret. She is easily the most fetching human he has ever seen. He finds her sadness irresistible.

Margaret Hildegard Atwood. To him it is like music, the name that has brought him back to his destiny, back to his mission on Earth after all this time. He will not fail again.

Alright then, thinks the Leader, brushing his scaly palms together briskly, work to be done! His crew backs away in a widening circle as the Leader rises from the ground, brings his knees to his chest and disappears.

Margaret wakes to find herself staring at the ceiling and trying to focus on a sound in her head, deep inside her ears. She has heard this sound before, maybe in a dream. Maybe she is dreaming right now. She tries to control her breathing so that she can hear the sound more clearly. She breathes slowly through her nose and something about this way of breathing seems to make her heart beat faster. The sound surfaces again: it is like a drone of bees, but there is a rhythm that travels a path of about twenty paces and then begins again; it is a winding loop of a song. She tries to turn up the volume with her brain and it seems to her that there are words murmured in unison, that the sound is a chant. She can hear the *f*'s and the *k*'s and maybe the compressed-air sound of a *th*. There is a pleasing, humming beauty to the sound and it makes her feel a terrible pull, a yearning in her heart and in her throat, as if she is about to cry or break into song and this is when she turns her eyes from the ceiling to the figure that is standing beside her bed.

Margaret can see the alien out of the corner of her eye but can't seem to turn her head toward him. Her body is asleep but her brain is awake. She grunts with frustration as she tries to sit up, to move her legs. Finally with great effort she rolls her cement head toward him and looks into his black, black eyes. She remembers that she has seen him before, in this very spot by her bed, that somehow he has helped her and that he will not eat her or steal her away. She will not be the subject of experiments. She waits for something to happen. The Leader leans down toward her and sits on the edge of the bed. He reaches out and cups Margaret's face in his hands. Her cheeks are hot and damp. He wants to appear as if every move is planned and perfectly natural. He does not want to appear frightened.

Margaret decides to stay calm and continue to wait him out. She cannot imagine what might happen next. She is concentrating on the feeling of the alien's skin, the way it is surprisingly dry and warm and papery like that of a snake. When she looks again at the alien's eyes, he tries to speak.

His voice is mechanical and strange and his words completely unintelligible, but they act as a signal. Margaret feels a painful crack in her chest. There is a tiny, hard kernel in her chest that may be all that is left of her heart and it is cracking painfully open. Something is released in Margaret's throat and she begins to crow and squeal, to roll out words she has never heard before. She doesn't recognize her own voice. She doesn't know what she is saying, what she is screaming. Tears are streaming down her face and her legs are rigid and trembling, her bare knees and ankles knocking against each other. A crazy stream of language rushes through her throat and out of her mouth.

The Leader sits as still as he can and waits for the wailing to stop. Finally, worn out, Margaret lays her head in the alien's lap and cries like a baby, her warm tears running onto his thighs. His skin smells like honey and something fresh and soapy, something like lime. She thinks that maybe she can feel his hard penis pressing against the back of her head, but is too tired to move away.

The Leader waits for a few minutes and then places Margaret's head carefully back onto her pillow.

He places his hand over her eyes.

"You will not remember this." He speaks these words directly into her ear in the perfect earthling voice of Donald Sutherland. That's more like it.

Margaret feels the bed drop away and falls into the perfect vacuum of deep sleep. The alarm clock, from its foreign position in the middle of the bedroom floor, signals the morning.

Three

Everyone carries a kernel of sadness

EVERYONE CARRIES A KERNEL OF SADNESS, even Donald Sutherland. That is why his voice sounds the way it does and that is why it is universally compelling (an excellent choice on the part of the Leader). Even that other Margaret Atwood has one – you can tell by her sharp wit and her crazy monotone delivery when she reads from her books.

Even his purple highness, Prince, carries a kernel of sadness. And yet he never loses his groove – you can find him on stage, on television, year after year, glowing and ageless in some ruffled silk concoction, making love to his guitar. Warren Zevon had one – you can hear it in every song, in every dying breath of that last album. And poor, sweet, clever Spalding Gray had one. Everyone knows that.

The Queen of England probably has one the size of Buckingham Palace, you can never tell.

It goes without saying that Margaret's mother and father and Marie the Christian and Lenny the Supervisor and every one of the aliens has one.

There is no escape.

The big bad wolf

YES, EVERYONE CARRIES A TINY kernel of sadness, even Brian.

Brian is an interesting case, though. He is completely unaware of his kernel – sadness is a feeling that he does not entertain. Though occasionally he does feel a certain tightness in his chest.

On this bright autumn morning, Brian sits in his office and contemplates his day while looking out the window at the flawless blue sky. Brian loves his office; it is the one place in the world that he feels is completely his own. He thinks of it as his little apartment, his bachelor pad, his lair. He has his favourite coffee mug here, his favourite rocks glass, his favourite brand of whiskey nestled in his desk drawer. He has a nice Oriental rug and expensive-looking dark furniture. There is a place to hang his coat and a rubber mat for his boots in the winter.

Brian has taken great joy in decorating his office in an entirely selfish way. It is a concession-free, negotiation-free zone. No womanly approval has been required.

On the walls, you will find only items that say something about Brian, as he would like to be seen by others. A photograph of Jack London, his childhood hero, tells you that he is an adventurer, a man of action. His various diplomas and awards, identically framed and hung together in a neat grid, demonstrate the extent and particular nature of his intelligence and success. Finally, Brian has hung a photograph of *Trans-Am Apocalypse No. 2* by John Scott right above his desk. *Trans-Am Apocalypse No. 2* is an installation piece that Brian has seen on display at the National Art Gallery.

The artist had scratched passages from the Book of Revelation into the paint of a black sports car. The entire car is covered in crazy warnings from the Bible. The idea had made Brian laugh. He liked the notion of Judgement roaring through the world in the form of a big, nasty, fast car. The photo has allowed him to start conversations and share a laugh with any number of difficult people that had entered his office over the years. (Brian had heard that the same artist had had a piece of his own skin surgically removed and tattooed with roses and a six-digit number to honour the memory of Nazi concentration camp victims. If memory served, the skin was mounted in a case and displayed in a gallery somewhere in Europe. This impressed Brian less. It seemed a bit obvious, a bit overwrought. To be honest, it made him feel a little queasy.)

Brian wants the Trans-Am to tell people a few things about him. He wants to suggest he knows something about both art *and* cars. More importantly, he wants to alert people to the fact that he will not be very careful with their feelings. He wants them to believe that he doesn't care what they think. Which – there can be no doubt – he does.

One of the many things that Brian will never tell anyone is that the big, black car has figured prominently in his most frequent daydream. He often sits in this very chair, looking out the window as he is now, and pictures himself descending upon the city in the Trans-Am of the Apocalypse. He rests his wrists on top of the steering wheel and watches the earth rise up slowly to meet him. The wheels are already spinning as they touch down. A great batman-like cape unfurls behind the car, miles long, casting a shadow on the faces of the sinners who stand in the streets, gazing up in awe. Brian tears through the city passing swift and merciless judgement on all he sees. *You. Not you. You and you. Not any of you. Not a chance.*

Yes, Brian loves his office.

Today Brian is thinking about Margaret and how he might get away with keeping most of their still jointly owned assets. He would like to keep most of the money and convince Margaret to forgive him and to be his friend, and maybe even sleep with him one more time. Wouldn't it be something for Margaret to be the other woman for once? He suspects that she is probably very lonely and therefore ripe for manipulation.

Though it is true that she has been sort of bitchy lately. Perhaps he should wait.

For the record, this is exactly what Brian thinks of Margaret. He thinks that she is boring. When they were married she never once did anything interesting that was her own idea. He thinks that as a woman Margaret has never capitalized on her assets. That ass never shaken, those breasts crushed into her 'minimizer' bra, smothered in sweaters. His kingdom for some cleavage! But no, Margaret was never so inclined. Or has not been for a very long time.

And she is cranky. She is weak and submissive and deserves what she has: a boring job, a shabby apartment and a surfeit of her own company. Brian thinks that Margaret had been dragging him down, that she was depressing. He also firmly believes that Margaret is still in love with him. Her snotty phone message does not fool him. In his experience women always pine for the men that reject them; it is rooted in their nature. Surely, it is from the time of the cave: the great, hairy man-beast that shows no interest must surely be superior and therefore a good genetic bet.

If you are wondering, as the aliens do, whether Brian's chronic infidelity troubles his conscience, it does not. Guilt has nothing to do with his kernel of sadness. In his view his behaviour is fair. He has always been generous and entertaining in his relationships and he has never been faithful. He is of the opinion that if his affairs remain undiscovered, then he has done his partner no harm. If his adventures are discovered then his partner, like any other human with a spine, has the option to stay or to go. It does not trouble him. People should do what makes them happy.

What would make Brian happy right now has to do with money. He has drawn up an agreement and a Joint Application for Divorce that he wants Margaret to sign. But this is not what he will tell her. What he will tell her (when she is less angry and even more lonesome) is that he will have these papers drawn up according to her wishes, that he will cover the costs entirely. They just have to agree on a few small things. He is counting on Margaret being what she has always been: passive and lazy and easily tricked. A pushover.

Brian takes a deep breath and spins his chair again toward the window. The sky is a bright, uniform blue and the leaves on the trees in the park below are tangerine orange. He scans the sky for a cloud and there is not a single one. He takes this as a sign that he is on the right track, that everything will come together as planned. The path in the park is dotted with young couples holding hands. These couples are, he suspects, part of the swarm of new university students that have recently descended upon the city, ready to embark on another year of adventure and higher learning. It happens every year. They are not only to be found in the park: they bumble slowly through the grocery stores, stand in front of dairy cases debating with roommates the merits of tabouleh versus hummus, yoghurt versus quark; they crowd the movie theatres and stop dead in the middle of sidewalks, apparently forgetting altogether where they are and where they were going. Brian can't stand them.

So, you might ask, what is this kernel of sadness that Brian carries? Is it really there? Though unusually difficult to detect, Brian's kernel is surprisingly common. It is the very ordinary kernel of very ordinary men: in his tiny, hollow wooden heart Brian suspects that he is not manly, that he is a coward; he suspects that he might be just a little bit funny-looking and that he is not strong enough to win a fight against most men he knows; he fears that women are on to him, that they laugh at him after he skulks away in the night. He fears that nobody really has ever loved him at all.

Not even a little bit.

Like so many humans, he fears that his essential self may be completely unlovable. It makes him want to tear a hole in the life of everyone he has ever met.

Your mama

MOTHERFUCKER. IT IS SUNDAY morning and Rose can't stop thinking about this word. She can't stop thinking about saying it out loud.

She forms the word silently with her lips, feeling each distinct sound: the smooth *m*, the sticky *th*, the unequivocally satisfying *f*. The growl at the end of each part: *rrr-rrr!* She is astonished at how this outrageous insult has become commonplace, part of so-called urban culture. It seems that motherfucker has replaced 'dude,' which she supposes replaced 'guy,' which probably replaced some-thing like 'fellow.' Quite a leap. What can it mean? What can it possibly mean when people call their *friends* motherfuckers? Has the term lost its profane meaning or does it represent some sort of terrible nihilist admission: that these days everyone is a motherfucker but some of them are loveable anyway? Hard to say. From her current position – far, far over the hill – she may never know.

Rose is, of course, a mother herself. She is the mother of our own dear Margaret Atwood. Margaret Atwood, the lesser, as she understands it.

It should be noted here that when Rose named her first and only child, she had been completely unaware of that other Margaret Atwood, her own exact contemporary; Margaret Atwood who, at the time of Margaret's birth in 1969, was making a name for herself as a poet of significance and was poised to loose upon the world her first novel, *The Edible Woman*. That Margaret Atwood had been flying well below Rose's radar. Even now, Rose thinks that her daughter exaggerates the degree of fame that her namesake enjoys for dramatic effect. All those years ago, Rose had named her girl Margaret because she had thought it a nice, balanced name: it was fancy enough to belong to a princess, but had a sensible quality about it. Not too hot; not too cold. Just right.

But *Hildegard*. The middle name, Hildegard, had been pure mischief on Rose's part. On the many occasions she has been asked about its provenance she has cheerfully informed people that no, the name did not come from any ancestor or family friend. With a completely straight face she has contended that it was just the prettiest name she had ever heard. It makes her laugh every time she thinks of it. The looks on their faces!

The truth of the matter, which she has not even disclosed to her husband, is that she felt the name provided her daughter with a very minor and necessary test of character. If she had any backbone at all, she would learn to like the name and defend it. She would invest some time in learning its history, its meaning. A little project. Rose had not realized, however, that she had saddled her daughter with an already problematic name. A double whammy.

"Listen," Rose had told a teenaged Margaret, "I grew up down the street from a kid named Paul Newman. No kidding. These things happen."

"Really."

"Really. There was a kid in my grade named Marlon Brando."

"That is not true."

"OK. There was no Marlon Brando, unfortunately. But Paul Newman is real. He lived right down the street."

"*How could you?*" she screamed. Then, turning to her father, "How could you *let* her?"

Ron had just smiled, given his wife a wink, and retreated to his shed. Sometimes, he had found, it was better to stay out of these things. Besides, as Margaret had always been fully aware, he wasn't in the business of letting – or not letting – Rose do anything. Hurricane Rose would do as she pleased.

Hurricane Rose

ROSE THE HURRICANE IS SITTING at her kitchen table, cooling coffee in hand, staring out the window at the rain, rain, rain, bastardly rain. *Motherfucking rain.* She mouths it silently. She has been sitting in this exact spot since 4:00 a.m., thinking about her daughter, thinking about how motherhood is never-ending; how, once begun, it never stops disturbing one's sleep. Her husband, Ron – the father – is having no such trouble. Rose can hear him snoring in the room adjacent. She can picture his thinning, feathery hair against the pillow, his stubbled cheek, his soft, ancient pyjamas. He will not smell great, but he will smell familiar. Spicy and sweaty and warm. She thinks about climbing back in there and cuddling up, staying in bed with him until the weather improves, sleeping it off until some idea comes to her, some way of getting through to her child who is too far away to grab by the shoulders and shake, shake, shake. Rose pads over to the bedroom door and looks in at her husband. He is exactly as expected: a dishevelled angel, deeply asleep. She thinks about how we all look like children when we sleep. Until we start to look like corpses. Wait for it. Any second now.

She returns to the kitchen table. Here Rose calculates the time difference between where she is and where her daughter is and realizes that Margaret is likely already at work. Though the sun (up there somewhere beyond the thick, grey, woolly storm clouds) has just risen here, Margaret will be up and gone. And she never takes Rose's calls when she is at work. She will have to wait until dinner time. An eternity. She feels caged. She wants to get things done; she wants to start making arrangements, but she is thwarted. She gets up and pours out her cold coffee, rinses the mug and sets it in the sink. She goes to the bathroom and brushes her teeth and then walks back to her bedroom, takes off her robe and then her nightie and then slides into bed beside her unsuspecting husband.

Without thinking, like diving into familiar water, she does exactly as she has done a thousand times: she pulls up close behind him so that her whole front is pressed against his whole back and she slides her hands over his chest, down over his belly, and under the waistband of his pyjamas. Ron doesn't open his eyes, maybe isn't even fully awake yet. He sighs as if all his dreams have come true and turns into her arms. Old Reliable, good old Ron. He has never let her down in this or any other way really. She kisses his sandpapery cheek, his ear, rolls over on top of him. They give each other conspirators' smiles as the rain splatters against the bedroom window.

How lucky she had been to find him.

When Rose met Ron Atwood, it was the summer of 1967, what Pierre Berton would later call "the last good year." For Rose that summer would mark the beginning of the best, most uncomplicated year of her life and the long-delayed launch of her adult life. She was twenty-eight years old and still, remarkably, living in her father's house.

(This can be explained. When Rose was still Rose Johnson, when she was a tiny girl of ten, her mother surprised everyone by dying of cancer. Deep in the flesh of Catherine Johnson's voluminous left breast, a lump of poison had been growing undetected for several years. By the time Catherine had brought the tumour to the attention of her doctor it had already sent out secret poison emissaries to every major port of her body. Rose was the oldest of three children; she had two younger brothers who became largely her responsibility in the wake of her mother's untimely departure. Rose's father, though he continued to get up every morning and go to work, to come home every evening, as he had done before, though he still cracked the odd joke, was never quite the same. So it was that Rose's girlhood was arrested and she turned her attention to the arduous and boring business of running a household.

The predicament of Rose's family – its vanished mother and single father – had had a specific and practical impact on the course of her life. She would not be able to leave home until both of her brothers were grown and out of the house and, even then, it would have meant leaving her father to fend for himself, which had seemed untenable. So, she had stayed on. She had been too busy for dating and she had stopped going to school by the time she was sixteen. She had, without really meaning to, become a housewife.)

By 1967, Rose's youngest brother, John, had moved out of the house four years earlier to go to school. The older of her two brothers, Sam, was already married and had a son. Rose had continued to live with her father as a kind of housekeeper, not really knowing what else to do. Until that bright, sunny summer day when Ron touched her shoulder from behind and everything changed.

At twenty-eight, Rose was still a beauty (and still a virgin). Her straight, brown hair was long and glossy and she had a winning, if distracted, smile. She had a buxom figure and perpetually rosy cheeks. On the day in question, Rose was standing outside the drugstore, completely bemused. She had come downtown to fill a prescription for her father, something for his blood pressure, and she thought she had come here on her bicycle but it seemed to have disappeared. She had placed it in the bike stand on the sidewalk in front of the drugstore, she was certain. It had not yet occurred to her that it might have been stolen.

Ron, a young pharmacist, had been staring out the shop window at Rose for some time. He stood behind the counter and he struggled with himself. She seemed to be in need of some help, didn't she? She had been standing there an awfully long time. But maybe he would be intruding. The breeze blew her skirt against her legs and he could see the perfect shape of her thigh. He headed for the door.

He walked up behind her and gently, not wanting to startle her, placed two fingers on her shoulder. Heat like magic seeped through the thin fabric of her dress, running through his fingers like an electrical current. He could feel it in his knees. (Human chemistry – the aliens can't get enough of this. Nothing in the universe compares. It makes them squirm with envy.)

"Can I help you with something?"

Rose turned to look at him, at his smooth dark beard and his kind dark eyes and, feeling utterly ridiculous and with ridiculous tears stinging her eyes, she said, "I can't find my bicycle."

And this is how the relatively late-flowering, long-lasting romance of Rose and Ron began. He was thirty-two and she, twenty-eight. They were married within the year. She was pregnant soon after. And they created a monster: a baby monster made of love that would never, ever let her sleep through the night again. A thirty-five-year-old monster that is separated from her husband, drinks too much and refuses to answer the phone.

Rose gently disentangles herself from her husband. She showers, dresses for the day and returns to the kitchen table having killed some time and in a slightly better mood. She pines for her daughter, for some comfort that everything will turn out alright again. For the mushy kernel of Rose's sadness is something to do with the terrible, bittersweet pull of motherhood. Motherhood, the motherfucker above all others: the feeling of always being the lifeguard on duty, of never having a moment's peace. Counting and counting and counting the precious, vexing little chicks to make sure all are accounted for. Rose believes that, except for that single unspoiled year, sandwiched between her father's house and her daughter's birth, that one year alone with her lovely husband, she cannot remember ever feeling at ease. She is always on stand-by. She wants to turn it off, but she can't. Duty calls. She can feel the motherfucking cape unfurling behind her as she rises from the table. Stand tall, mother! Fly!

The terrible, bittersweet pull

STUPID BABIES. SOMETIMES she feels like everywhere she looks there are babies. Fat ones like miniature sumo wrestlers, rolls of fat oozing over their wrists onto their hands, over their ankles onto their fat feet. As if they are overinflated, overstuffed. Fat, boneless, drooling human milk-sponges. Doorstop babies. Or the skinny ones, their red skin loose on their tiny bodies, wrinkling in their elbow creases and behind the knees, their heads unthinkably small, the size of oranges or little hairy baseballs. They look underdone or like they are melting. Like a baby doll left in the rear window of the car too long.

Gross.

And yet the world swoons and fawns over babies.

Margaret's co-worker, Vanessa, has brought her baby to the office for a visit and everyone is gathered around, jabbering like monkeys. Margaret is lurking at the edges of the crowd trying to devise the best strategy for impersonating a human female, without inviting too much attention, without risking contact with the baby itself.

There is the problem of concealing her distaste for babies and also there is the problem of Vanessa. Vanessa is probably the closest thing that Margaret has to a friend. They are the same age, of the same view about their work and have been allies at the office for more than ten years. They have gossiped, carped, and shared sidelong glances in meetings. They have drained bottles of wine together while Vanessa listened patiently to Margaret's many complaints about her husband. But Margaret is pretty sure that Vanessa has had enough of her now, has decided she is not worth the effort. There have been too many unreturned phone calls. Too many times, Margaret has pretended not to see her on the street. She knows that for too long, Vanessa has felt like the entertainment in the relationship, constantly tap dancing to rouse Margaret from her seemingly endless funk.

And now she is busy entertaining her offspring.

Margaret looks at her friend and cannot quite believe the change in her. Her face is pudgy and soft and her eyes are all shiny and wet. Cocker spaniel eyes. There is something crusty and white on her shoulder and her breasts are comically huge, puffing out the front of her billowy flowered tunic. She is wearing stretch pants and Birkenstocks. None of this squares with Margaret's memory of her friend, who previously contended that t-shirts were not suitable for wearing outside the house and was embarrassed to be seen in flat shoes. She would not have believed it if she hadn't seen it with her own eyes: Vanessa has been motherized.

And now the schlumpy Madonna looks up from her baby and fixes Margaret in her laser-eyed gaze. She points at her and mouths the word, "*Asshole.*"

Margaret blushes and looks at her feet, coughing and laughing at the same time.

This almost reminds her of why she had liked Vanessa in the first place, somewhere once upon a time, back when she had liked anyone at all. She hopes that nobody has noticed this exchange between them, but she needn't have worried. All eyes are on the chubby, pink-cheeked star of the show, a baby girl named Veronica. She burbles and squeals, she belches and blows spit bubbles and furrows her brow. The crowd goes wild. Margaret nods at her friend, acknowledging that, yes, she is an asshole, and turns away to retreat to her desk.

Ten minutes later, Vanessa and her baby are filling the doorway of Margaret's cubicle. Two sets of eyes, same shape, same colour. Two eyes in a big head, two eyes in a small head, glaring.

"So, what the hell? You don't need friends now? You think I don't need a friend?" Baby Veronica raises an eyebrow at Margaret and lets something that looks like vanilla pudding spill out of her mouth and over her chin. Vanessa promptly wipes it off with the hem of the baby's badly stained t-shirt, revealing her plump little belly. "I'm sick of chasing you, Margaret. I feel like a chump."

"So stop."

"What?"

"So stop chasing me." Margaret feels small and deflated. She longs to return to her boring work and to be left in peace.

"Don't you care even a little bit about my life? About what might be going on with me?"

"I want to care, Vanessa. I want to be a good friend but I just don't have the energy for it."

"Because you're really busy, right? You're just worn right out from what exactly? From working precisely seven and a half hours a day and doing nothing else at all? Is that what's making you so tired?"

Margaret takes a deep breath. "I'm getting divorced. I think my mother is coming to visit."

"Whatever." The baby starts to hiccup and cry and Vanessa hoists her upright over her shoulder and starts bouncing her up and down. Margaret wants to cry, too, but there are no tears right now, only dust. Crusty old dust inside her crusty old face.

"I have to go. If you want to see me, call me. I'm done calling you for now."

"OK," says Margaret, even though her friend is already gone, flip-flopping down the corridor in her sandals. "Fine, then."

That evening, Margaret is sitting on the couch eating mushroom egg foo-yung out of the carton, soon to be followed by four crispy, greasy egg rolls dunked in plum sauce. It is the special monthly glutton time. Her uterus feels like a hard rubber ball low in her abdomen, pulsing with pain. She is wearing giant sweat pants with a hot water bottle shoved down the front. The magic of womanhood. Every month is more painful and bloody than the last. It is as if her body is angry with her, as if it is trying to send a message that she refuses to receive. She wonders why it doesn't give up, already. Nothing is going to grow in there, nothing ever has.

The thought of it almost puts her off her egg roll.

It is interfering with her ability to enjoy the TV show she is watching about a woman whose face has been eaten off by a bear.

Margaret guesses that she grew up wanting babies, like most other girls, but this is another thread she has lost. She didn't lose it all at once, though. Before she was married, she had very effectively conditioned herself to see pregnancy as the worst possible outcome; every time her period was late she was filled with terror. Then, when she and Brian were first married, she had allowed herself the fantasy of a small family. One curly-headed, Brian-like baby, maybe a miniature baby Margaret. Something to anchor her husband in place, something to fill the cavity in her own chest. An excuse to stay home from work for a year or two.

But, Brian had, not surprisingly, been evasive about parenthood from the beginning. He had avoided the subject expertly. She had been convinced that news of impending fatherhood would have sent him running for the hills. And she was probably right. Not that he had stuck around anyway, and what was she left with now?

Zip. Nada.

Would she be happier now if she had had a child? Probably not. Just busier and poorer and more bitter, if that were possible. Would she find her own baby less disgusting than other people's babies? She is not convinced. She can't shake the idea that there is something invasive about pregnancy, the foetus like a parasite or a tumour growing in there.

Pushing another dripping egg roll into her mouth, Margaret thinks that this whole fertile phase of her life will likely be over before she ever has sex again, anyway. If there is a god. Which she is pretty sure there isn't.

The spiritual guide

HERE IS SOMEONE WHO BELIEVES in God with her whole beaming heart: perfect Marie the snitch.

Marie loves Jesus so much it gives her a stomach ache sometimes. She loves him the way ladies of a certain age love Tom Jones. It is the kind of love that makes you clasp your hands together beneath your chin and catch your breath. She's got the joy, joy, joy, joy down in her heart, down in her heart to stay!

The sweet love of Jesus, which Marie knows is available to everyone who accepts it, has not, however, prevented her from developing her own kernel of sadness. This is different from the sadness she carries on the outside, on her sleeve. Everyone knows that she is sad for sinners that have not found Jesus; she is sad for children who starve and for people who have no home. She is sad about the increasing cheapness and depravity of our culture as seen on TV. Marie is sad for all the suffering in the world, but she knows it is only in this world that we suffer. In the next one there will be comfort and peace.

The aliens know all about Marie and they do not scoff at her simple faith. They are filled with admiration. Marie, of all the humans they know, has the clearest conscience and the calmest heart. And she conducts herself, for the most part, with selfless kindness. In general, the aliens find that religious humans, the ones that are true believers, do not twist in the wind the way other humans do. They have direction.

Marie feels she has much to be thankful for. She is a healthy young woman with a good, honest job; she was raised by loving Christian parents who provided her with everything she needed. (Marie still lives with her parents and plans to stay with them until, with their blessing, she gets married.) She sees evil all around her but it does not tempt her. She is strong. She is aware of people ignoring the teachings of Jesus, making the wrong decisions all the time, but she knows it is not her place to judge. A day will come and judgements will be made and they will not be made by Men.

Marie knows why humans are not meant to judge each other – it is because we are simply not qualified. Though it seems mostly clear to Marie what is right and what is wrong, sometimes people need guidance. On some occasions you pray for direction and you get it; but some things you can never quite figure out. Which brings us a little closer to the source of Marie's sadness. It is something she cannot figure out, something about which God has given her no clear direction, something she can never tell her parents.

When Marie was thirteen years old, she went on a bus trip to a stadium in a nearby city where an American preacher was holding a 'forum for youth.' The day-long event featured bible studies, discussion groups, a long talk from the preacher himself about the preciousness of chastity, and concluded with an uncommonly wholesome party, complete with non-alcoholic beverages and a performance by a Christian rock band. Young Marie felt it was quite a grown-up event and had been very surprised that her parents had let her come, even with the battalion of chaperones from their church.

One of these chaperones was named Tom Francis and, as he often said, he had a special place in his heart for Marie. He said he could see the love of Jesus shining in her eyes. He said that only God could make such a beautiful and innocent creature. Marie found Tom to be quite unlike any other adult she knew. He wore jeans and sneakers and funny t-shirts. He had sandy hair and blue eyes and looked kind of like a lifeguard. (Tom was not a lifeguard. In fact, he worked at a factory that made wooden skids.) In his spare time, Tom ran a Christian DJ business providing entertainment for weddings, dances and parties. But, he preferred to work with the youth of the church. It was his calling.

And of all the young people he had ever seen, Marie was the one Tom felt called to mentor. He zeroed in on her that day at the Virgins for Christ forum, or whatever it was called, and introduced himself. They sat on the ground and talked about their lives. Tom said that sharing feelings with another Christian lightened the heart so that God could give clearer direction. He said that it was natural for teenagers to have difficulty talking to their parents. He told Marie that if she would let him he would like to be her spiritual guide – the teen years could be a difficult and confusing time, especially for Christians. If she wanted him to he would happily counsel her when she was in need. Marie felt so grateful to have someone to talk to, who would keep her secrets. She felt special to have been chosen.

"Don't be a stranger!" said Tom.

Marie thought this was funny: "But we *are* strangers! I just met you!" She knew this was not quite true. She had seen Tom many times at church but today was the first time she had really talked to him alone.

"That will never be true again, Marie. We're friends now. Better than friends. We're united in Christ. There's something very special happening between you and me."

"I guess so," said Marie. "We better get going or we'll miss the bus." She didn't know what time it was, but she could see that most of the kids and chaperones were filtering out the exits toward the rows of yellow-orange school buses in the parking lot. She recognized some of the grown-ups from her church looking over their shoulders at her and she started to feel nervous.

"Did you ever think, Marie, that some people are half angels? Some people are so good and sweet that their feet are just a little bit lighter on the earth than other people's?"

"No!" She was blushing now. She was anxious to leave, but wanted to hear what he would say next. She started walking backward in front of him toward the exit. "I don't think that can be true."

"I know it's true, Marie. The first time I saw you in church, sitting there with your parents, your pretty face turned up toward heaven, your hair shining like gold, I knew I was seeing an angel from God. I went home, Marie, and I prayed. Maybe you don't believe me."

"I believe you."

"I prayed to God and said, 'Lord, what do you want me to do? Why did you show me this girl?' And that night I had a dream that Jesus came to me and said, 'Take this perfect girl and guide her. Make sure she is not corrupted.' And I knew that I would. That we would be great friends, Marie. And now we are! Hallelujah!" He laughed and grabbed both of her hands and she laughed, too. And then she broke away and ran for the buses as fast as she could.

Sweaty and flushed, she scrambled into a seat near the back of the bus. She pressed her hot forehead against the cool glass of the window. As the bus pulled away, she looked up to see Tom swaying down the aisle of the bus toward her. He steadied himself against a seat for a second and ran his hand through his shaggy hair. Marie thought maybe it was Tom who was a half angel because she thought she could see light around him, just a little bit of golden light. He winked and then stumbled forward into the seat beside her.

Marie thought this was the best event she had ever been to. She couldn't wait to tell her parents all about it.

As the bus rumbled down the long, straight highway, Marie closed her eyes and thanked God for watching over her and for sending her a guide. Her head was so heavy that she could barely hold it up. She let her cheek rest against his shoulder, against the thin, soft cotton of his t-shirt, and fell asleep like a baby.

Like the good, little angel girl she was.

The precious treasure

THE MORE MARIE GOT TO KNOW Tom the more she liked him and the more she wanted to spend time with him. He started to come to her parents' house on a more or less weekly basis and once in a while he would take Marie out for ice cream or to a church event. He suggested to Marie's parents that she could help him with his duties as the church treasurer.

In her capacity as Assistant Treasurer, Marie accompanied Tom to many committee meetings, where she dutifully took minutes. Sometimes, on the odd Saturday or weekday evening, Tom and Marie would meet at the church office to go over accounts and make plans for fundraisers. They spent more time, however, roaming around the deserted church and talking about their feelings.

Marie loved the church when it was empty. The plain pews were the shiniest blond wood anyone could imagine and they swept back from the pulpit in great fans on either side of the aisle. The carpet was blood red and the windows were stained glass. There was a balcony at the back with more pews, she supposed for when all the other pews were full, though she had never seen anyone sitting there. She liked to go up there and look down on the church, to look at this familiar place from a new angle. Sometimes she even went up to the front of the church and stood at the pulpit to see what things looked like from the pastor's point of view, with the choir loft behind him and the congregation before him. It gave her a strange and excited feeling.

There were also places that she had never imagined. There was the tiny, shabby office in the basement, packed with paper and filing cabinets and thumbtacked messages and at the top of some stairs and up a ladder, there was the bell tower. The desire to ring the bell was terrifying and unbearable. There was a creepy storage room filled with robes, crucifixes, brass and wooden candle holders. Sometimes when she and Tom were at the church in the evening he would turn all the lights off and they would play hide-

and-seek. Marie had never been more frightened or laughed so hard in all her life.

She loved being found.

There were moments so beautiful, so like dreams, that she would never forget them. One night in the pitch-black church she found her way very quietly up all the flights of stairs to the ladder leading to the small opening in the ceiling that led to the bell tower. She climbed up the ladder, pulled herself up and tiptoed to a dark corner and pressed her back into it. Her breathing was heavy, amplified, the sound bouncing off the cold stone. From her corner Marie looked up at the single, enormous bell suspended at the top of the tower. Around its silhouette she could see the night sky. It was the darkest violet and sparkled silver with stars and the bell was black as ink. She was sweaty from running around the musty church and the cool fresh air that flowed through the tower was velvet on her skin. She will never forget how lucky she felt. Like she was doing something that no one was ever allowed to do.

Then things started to change between Marie and Tom. The aliens cannot understand why things so often go this way when a grown man spends too much time alone with an adolescent girl (or boy), but it surely does. Here on earth, it is a wretched and predictable phenomenon. They suppose it is because children are easy to trick.

In the beginning, Tom and Marie had talked about everything and a lot about Jesus. Then as time went by the focus was increasingly on the subject of chastity. Tom commended Marie for guarding her virginity like the precious treasure that it was. He warned Marie to stay away from boys. If she wanted to kiss someone, she could kiss him. She could practice! He surely would never tell anyone. It was better that she learned with him where she was safe.

He could show her the kind of touching that was sinning and the kind that was not. It was just a way of being close to each other, of honouring the beauty of their bodies, created by God.

At the time, she thought that she had a lot to thank Tom for.

Now that she was a grown woman and had some idea of what

it meant for a thirty-two-year-old man to have such a relationship with a thirteen-year-old girl, she was beginning to see things differently.

These days, the kernel in her chest ached until her breath stuck in her lungs.

The variety of angels

It is lunch time at the button factory and Margaret is hiding at the art gallery again. As part of her plan to avoid speaking to any of her co-workers ever again she has a rotational list of hiding places in which to spend her lunch hour – food courts, parks, libraries and courtyards – but the art gallery is by far her favourite. It is virtually empty all the time and very close to silent. Bored security guards shuffle from room to climate-controlled room and never speak to anyone, not even each other. Some of them have noted Margaret's frequent visits, but they don't care about her. They are not looking at the paintings, either; they just shuffle around, dreaming their own waking dreams, hoping against hope that the day will pass quickly.

But days never pass quickly at the art gallery. This on account of all the old, old things that hang here, dragging the hands of the clock backward. Churches are like this, too: every minute lasts for two or three. Unless you are under twenty-five years old. Then every minute is an eternity.

Margaret is content to let time unwind slowly. She will wait until precisely ten minutes before the hour and then walk slowly back to the office. She times her return so that she arrives about two minutes after most people have gone back to their desks and have settled in to work for the afternoon. She sits on a leatherette bench in the middle of a large room in the corner of the top floor of the gallery and chews on the peanut butter sandwich she has smuggled in with her. There is not another visitor in sight. She can hear signs of a security guard in the next room: intermittent throat clearing and the crackle of a walkie-talkie. She is prepared to shove the entire remainder of her sandwich into her mouth should she hear footsteps approaching.

Watching Margaret eat her sandwich are the many shining eyes of saints and angels. The saints in their green or red or blue robes encrusted with jewels and shot through with gold, heads topped with haloes; the angels hanging like plump grapes in the sky, or looming out of the shadows like terrifying man-sized birds of prey. There is an archangel standing on the head of a cloven-hoofed devil and there are angels bearing a red-caped bishop aloft on a magic carpet of clouds. There are angels that are only baby heads with wings sprouting out of the place where their ears should be. Such a variety of angels, such a strange assortment of creatures. Not to mention the dragons and demons and the risen dead; the punctured, flayed and scalped.

But these are not the ones that keep Margaret coming to the gallery.

That creature is in the next room.

Hanging by itself at the far end of the next room is the painting Margaret visits last every time she comes here. It is nine feet high and four feet wide. Big enough that if you sit right in front of it you can imagine yourself inside it. If she gets close enough it feels like the white stallion is towering above her, about to trample her. She can look up into its black flaring nostrils. Astride the steed is St. James the Greater, red hair and beard shining in the sunlight, his brown eyes turned toward heaven. As if by accident, his lowered sword is beheading the soldier toppling over at his right foot. If you look through the legs of the horse you can see the trail of dead he is leaving in his wake. In his left hand St. James holds a white flag with a brilliant orange stripe and it ripples behind him into the distance. If this scene were to come to life, the flag would be at least fifty feet long. It flies away, deep into the dreamy blue sky of the painting.

This is a scene of glory, of triumph. Margaret doesn't want to be whisked away by this hero on his white horse; she wants to become him. She wants to feel victorious. She wants to win something in her life, just once. She dares to dream of it only for as long as she sits in front of the painting. She dreams of rising up and flying through the air like the long tail of that bright saffron flag.

But it seems like such a long climb out of this hole, up to the podium, up onto that white horse. This deep, dark hole. There is no glory for proofreaders, no prize for wallowing. She chokes down the last bite of her sandwich, smoothes out the crumb-filled plastic bag and leaves it there on the bench, a memento for the guards.

The calling card of The Wallower.

Super power

WHENEVER MARIE FEELS SORRY for herself, she finds it helpful to concentrate on the suffering of Jesus. If she does it for long enough it always reveals her own suffering as the trifle it really is.

She thinks of Jesus on the cross in the hot sun. How sore and parched his throat must have been. She thinks of the horrible sickening ache in the fine, laced bones of his feet. How the pain must have shot through him from all directions: from the wound in his side, from his hands and feet, from the stinging ludicrous crown on his head. She tries to imagine what happens to the mind under such conditions. Did Jesus imagine himself outside of the broken husk of his human body? Did he imagine himself passing out of the cage of his chest and floating into the sky to be with the Holy Father? Or did he focus on the matter at hand: did he do his best to feel every pulse of terrible pain because he knew that he was taking pain away from his followers, that because he endured this pain, we would all be saved? Marie knows that he looked into the eyes of those who mocked him and thought, "I am doing this for you, even though you despise me."

Why would Jesus care about mockery when he knew he was the son of God and that he was saving the world?

To be mocked was the lot of Christians in this debased world, Marie knows that. She has been mocked all her life. She had been teased for wearing skirts to school instead of jeans, for not wearing make-up and not going to dances and not swearing. She had been teased about her shoes and her haircut and her propensity for blushing; she had been teased for her general ignorance of pop culture. Marie remembers a fall day outside the high school when she had explained to some of her classmates why movies about aliens were anti-Christian and why Halloween was really about Satan. This had been the tipping point. From that day forth, there was no limit to other kids' disdain for Marie. They laughed in her face wherever she turned.

But Marie had withstood these tests.

What did she care what a bunch of hooligans at school thought?

She would be rewarded in the next life.

Yes, Marie was an old hand at being mocked. She could let it ride. What she could not abide, however, was when people mocked the suffering of Christ. Mocking Christians was one thing; mocking the Lord was another. She was not stupid either. She knew what people were up to. People like Margaret. She knew that a certain breed of educated and cynical people thought it was cutting edge to be so *politically incorrect*. She felt sorry for people who were so shallow and bored and self-involved.

Not sorry enough, though.

That day when Margaret had made her joke at the photocopier, only two weeks after Marie had started her new job, she knew what had to be done. She knew what her rights were and she did not intend to let her workplace become as poisonous as her high school had been.

She had felt righteous and grown-up when she walked into Lenny's office.

She felt the power.

The saddest elf

Lenny had cringed as Marie laid out her complaint before him. Christ, he thought, there was always something! Always some damn thing.

Lenny had a staff of fourteen people working for him and not a single one of them was ever happy. For twenty-five years of his meaningless career, Lenny had wanted to be in charge. He had thought of little else. It had consumed him like a teenage crush. He had been certain that if he followed the rules, if he worked hard enough, he would achieve his goal. He would sit in a real office with a door that closed, get paid more money, and tell people what they could and could not do. Well, guess what? Management stunk. It reeked like garbage in August. It had the distinct aroma of people and their endless *issues*. Issuing forth. An endless trail of human emotional slime.

He had hated it from the beginning.

It seemed to him that along with the marginal increase in salary, he collected more blame for more things and had to babysit a bunch of grown-up whiners (all of whom supposed themselves smarter than him and more worthy of his job). It was beginning to wear him down.

And Margaret Atwood would be the death of him.

Margaret presented a special challenge for Lenny. She was both his best and his worst employee. She was by far the most effective of workers – punctual, thorough, fast. She was not, though, what you might call a team player. Lenny had learned through his many (and mostly useless) management courses that a large part of his job was to keep people happy and engaged and feeling like they belonged to a *winning team*. Margaret was no part of any team. She declined all social invitations. She stalked through the corridors of the office and – Lenny swore – she sprouted quills at the sight of a co-worker.

She looked upon Lenny with utter disdain. And now this.

Lenny is a little tiny man, elf-like. He has a closely trimmed elf beard and twinkling elf eyes. And he is rumpled and creased. His pants and shirts are creased, his hands are corrugated, his neck and face and his increasingly visible scalp are all creased. There are lines within creases within craters. But this is recent. Before taking this job, he was only small and awkward. Now he has collapsed into himself like an accordion. He is like the sad damp skin of a deflated balloon. He is much less than half a man. He has always felt this way on the inside, but now it shows on the outside.

All his life Lenny had been convinced that a woman would never find him physically attractive, so he had worked on his patter: his theory had been that a good salesman could sell anything, even his substandard self. In high school he had practiced on every girl who would look his way. He would see how long he could keep a girl talking to him, how many times he could make her laugh. He had been determined to be warm and funny and charming and sure enough he had convinced a woman, now his wife, to love him.

Sometimes Lenny leans back in his chair in his cramped, beige office, the door closed against the irritating hordes, and lets the image of seventeen-year-old Sharlene Wilson float into his mind. She had been as plump and rosy as a girl could be, with long, sandy hair and freckles. Her eyelashes and eyebrows were invisible, which gave her a strange, gauzy look. He remembers the first time he saw Sharlene naked. It had been the first time he had seen any girl naked and it had broken his heart, she was so beautiful. He remembers how white her skin was and how amazingly soft; he remembers her pale pink nipples and the red creases pressed into her belly by her too-tight jeans. Lenny remembers, with a painful, helpless stab of desire, the bristling sandy hair between her legs. He had felt like a king to be loved by such a creature.

Though she didn't seem to love him so much now. Lenny and Sharlene have not had sex in more than seven years and Sharlene has told him that she does not intend to ever do it again so he should just forget about it. She has had enough and now she wants some peace. Lenny cannot quite believe that she means this. Surely, she will come around. Every night, as Lenny gazes at his sleeping wife, who now weighs well over three hundred pounds, he is still overcome by the beauty of her face. She does not sneer when she is sleeping or tell him to go to hell. She just lays there, warm and fleshy and innocent as a baby. Oh, how he longs to nuzzle into the heat of her! But he knows better.

Also inhabiting Lenny's little house are his two teenage daughters, Becky and Lisa. They smoke and argue and listen to loud music and leave dirty clothes and towels everywhere. Lenny loves them and worries about them and cleans up their messes. And they, too, tell him to go to hell on a regular basis.

Oh, the humiliations that have been visited upon him by Becky and Lisa! What plots and scams have been devised to undo him! There are too many to tell, really, but this recent incident will be sufficient to demonstrate the terrible power of these girls, these human jackals with ponytails. It happened about two weeks before Marie walked into Lenny's office and told him the sad story of Margaret Atwood making a spectacle of herself at the photocopier.

Lenny is at home, collapsed in a rumpled lump on his rumpled couch. He is watching a dating show on television and is trying to empty his mind of everything but the pretty girls on the screen. He is trying to inhabit the body of the handsome young man whose task it is to choose one of these girls for a special date. Lenny would take any of them on a special date, even though he doesn't really know what it means to go on a 'special date.' To be perfectly honest, he would take any girl in the world on a any kind of date.

On the couch, Lenny is flanked by his two daughters. He can feel them looking at him or looking through him at each other, but he is trying to block this: he is the bachelor on TV. Becky, his oldest, sits to his left. She is wearing a very tight fuchsia terry-cloth tracksuit. The top rides up to reveal her smooth, fat, round belly. An artificial diamond is suspended from a ring in her navel. Her younger and slightly more evil sister, Lisa, is regarding her father with disgust. Her curly, blonde hair is pulled tightly up into a grapefruit-sized pompom on top of her head. She is wearing a great deal of navy-blue eyeliner. She extends her leg and shoves at her father's thigh with a slippered foot.

Lisa: "Dad, you look tired and old. Oh my god, your skin is *yellow*. What's the matter with you?"

Becky: "Totally."

Lenny tries hard not to listen to them, but with every syllable, Lisa is kicking his thigh. The jostling makes it hard to focus on the show.

Lisa: "You know what we should do? We should highlight your hair!"

Becky: "Wicked."

So the terrible idea was spawned and gained momentum. The girls told Lenny that highlighting his hair would make him look younger, less tired. It would improve his skin tone and brighten the colour of his eyes. It might even make him look taller (this delivered by Becky, through a barely stifled snicker). Lenny began to picture himself on television with his new and better hair. As usual, he was putty in their hands.

This is how Lenny found himself grimacing in his office with shocks of his mouse-brown hair bleached lemon-yellow, listening to the complaint of the lovely young Marie. That this beautiful young woman that he desired (as he found himself desiring all young women these days) should have to see him like this was very sad. He felt sorely exposed. It felt like the air was burning his face. But this humiliation was only a drop in the great, deep well of Lenny's sadness.

It was not the saddest part by far.

The saddest part was this: when his daughters were doing his hair, when they were touching his sad, old head, when they were washing the stinging dye off his scalp, he had allowed himself to think that maybe they loved him.

Maybe his beautiful horrible daughters had some small feeling of fondness for their father after all.

This tender, elf-sized shred of hope, blown entirely away – this begins to describe the darkest depths of the hole that Lenny's adult heart has become.

It makes him want to cry like a baby.

Switchin' to glide

AND SPEAKING OF FATHERS, who is this? Who is this sitting quietly as an egg? Who is this plain egg wrapped in a plain sweater, sitting in a soft chair in a quiet room in a quiet house on a quiet street? Can you guess? Probably not.

This egg is Ron Atwood, husband of Rose, father of Margaret, retired pharmacist, sixty-nine years old. Do eggs have kernels? It is hard to tell. Based on what we know so far about Ron and Rose and Margaret, you might be tempted to assume that he is disappointed in his life, that he feels something is missing. You might think that he is overwhelmed by his wife or that he feels small. You might think that Ron Atwood had a secret wish to be something better, bigger, nastier, more exciting. Yet none of this is true.

Ron Atwood is one of those rare humans who is truly at peace. Ron feels that for his entire youth he yearned for things – to leave his parents' home, to make his own way in the world, to find love and the comfort of a home – and his yearning was rewarded with the very things he wished for. Simply put, he is a satisfied man.

Let's reach back a little into the small bungalow of Ron's childhood. It is Saturday and Ron's mother is in the kitchen. Ron's five brothers and sisters are running in and out of the house like ants, full of zigzagging purpose. You will see Ron, the smallest one, in the sun-baked driveway. He is building something out of scraps of wood and plastic found in the shed. This is what you will see. But what you will *hear* is Ron's father, Chuck. Chuck, who is a skilled auto mechanic and general handyman, likes to stride through the house hollering questions. Questions like: "What the hell is the matter with you?" and "Why the hell would you want to do it that way?" and "Why are you so stupid?".

Little Ron finds that his father's voice does not seem quite so loud when you are outside the small house, even if he is close to you. Inside, the sound bounces off the wall and back at you; outside it disperses. It floats up into the air with the clouds and fades away. For this reason, when his father is home, Ron spends most of his time out of doors. In the yard and in the shed, he can find hundreds of things to do: he collects worms, digs up and transplants dandelions, builds miniature towns, makes tiny landscapes. He is careful to always clean up his messes, to eradicate all evidence of his pursuits, so as not to cause any trouble. In this way, he navigated his childhood.

You might say that Ron's decision to study pharmacology was a controversial one. To be a pharmacist was a career unlike any of those chosen by his siblings and seemed, to Ron's father, to be a suspiciously fussy and exacting kind of work. Gay, almost. Through high school, Ron worked part-time and summers in his local pharmacy. He stocked shelves and worked the cash. He mopped the floor after closing time and cleaned the counters and the sinks. The work had many advantages: it kept him away from home and his father most waking hours; his boss was quiet and kind and paid him well; and many girls came to the drugstore every day. Ron watched the girls and women come and go, all day long. They bought candy and mints and sanitary pads and cough medicine and they filled prescriptions. Their prescriptions told so many sad stories! Stories of pain and suffering, of love and betrayal, of shame, shame, shame. There were things he had been previously aware of – pregnancies, sexually transmitted diseases, depression – and those he had never really considered: excessive facial hair, diet pill addiction, obsessive hair-pulling. You could spend your whole life worrying about girls and their astounding variety of problems. Ron treasured his privilege. And he fed his bank account and filled out applications for universities as far away from his home as he could manage.

Ron Atwood's sweetest memory is not the day he first saw Rose and it is not the birth of his only daughter, though both of those are sweet enough. Ron's sweetest memory is of the day that he moved into a small room in a big city, a couple of weeks before his first term at university. His room was cramped and its walls were painted a dark, glistening brown. It was tucked in the attic of a great, ranging rooming house run by a stern old woman named Gladys. Each day, in that time before his first term of school started, Ron would get up and wash, go downstairs and eat breakfast with ten other young men – usually porridge and fruit and coffee. He would spend the day walking around the city, trying to get to know bus routes and neighbourhoods, visiting the library. He would walk around the university and try to memorize the names of the buildings and would daydream about classes, trying to imagine exactly how they would be. Then he would return to the rooming house, eat his dinner quietly and retire to his room.

All alone in his brown room, Ron would lay on his bed and gaze at the ceiling and watch the light change as the sun went down. He would not turn on the lights and he would not make a sound. He would lie there and think of the pretty girls in the drugstore and their dark, dark secrets. He would imagine ways that he could save them. A pill, an ointment, a gentle word of comfort from Ron the Pharmacist of the Future and all their problems would evaporate.

He would lie there, alone with his thoughts and savour the liberty of being alone with his thoughts. No chance of his father thundering through the door to ask him what the hell he was doing. This was the moment of his greatest happiness. Ron had known that he was at the beginning of a path along which all his humble dreams would come true.

And they did, in fact, come true. He had run a thriving business where he had come to the aid of many women, as well as men and children. He had found his match in crazy Rose and they had raised a crazy – though in a very different way – daughter, Margaret.

And here he is, sixty-nine years old, a quiet egg of a man in the middle of his slightly untidy – his wife having a hurricane quality – but paid-for house. Rose keeps herself busy with her friends. His pretty and clever daughter has moved far away. Now that he is retired, he can spend his day in whatever boring and pleasant manner he wishes. If he is feeling social, he chats with the neighbours, plays the odd game of cards. If he is in a more solitary mood, he turns his attention to his many building projects.

The house and yard are filled with his benches and planters and end tables. And bird houses. He has built a city of birdhouses of various sizes and colours, hoping to attract various sizes and colours of birds. Some are tucked away in the bushes for the shy birds; some stand tall in the middle of the grass. Ron likes to sit on the back porch listening to the wind rustling in the trees, watching the mostly small, mostly brown birds dart in and out of the little houses, scattering seeds all over the lawn.

He has seen a duck or two wander out of the bushes at the back of the yard and then stagger back out again, finding themselves a little too far from the pond down the road. And once, as the sun was setting, he had seen a tall blue heron standing motionless on the peak of his neighbour's roof like a massive weathervane, the bird's silhouette so sharp against the rosy sky, it looked like it was cut from tin. It stopped his breathing to see it. He had wanted to call to Rose, but could only stare and wait until finally the bird ruffled and straightened up, stretched its wings, and made its awkward, gangly ascent into the sky, long legs trailing behind. He can still remember the feeling in his chest, a lifting and expanding feeling, euphoric, as though he, too, were rising up into the soft evening air above his neighbourhood. Sheer delight.

So what, you might ask, is the kernel of sadness in this perfectly contented man?

The truth is that it is very small and, at this late date, virtually dissolved in the warm, doughy tissue of his big, soft heart. It is very small and it is only this. Almost every time he did a kind thing for his daughter when she was a baby or a child, every time he picked her up or stroked her hair or told her how wonderful she was, he would feel a tiny sting and the sting was this: Ron Atwood wondered why his own father couldn't have been just a little bit nicer. What would it have cost him? Didn't he have the same piece of dough in his chest as the rest of us? Didn't his children tug at it just a little?

Ron will never know the answers to these questions. His

father is long dead. He had never bothered to have any kind of conversation with Chuck as an adult and for this he feels no regret. He knows it would have gotten him nowhere. He does not dwell on it. He has switched to glide.

Not easy being green

THE LEADER IS TAKING THE NIGHT off. He has made himself practically invisible and is pacing the perimeter of the roof of an office tower, the tallest one he could find. If you could get up there, if you could get past the night shift security guards, up the elevator, through the doors to the staircase without setting off the alarm; if you could get all the way up to the roof and step out into the frosty night air, you might notice something. You might notice small flashes of orange light like fireflies. They are here. Then over there. Then gone. You would never guess it was him, but it is the one and only: the sad and fatigued Leader of the aliens, the human being *manqué*.

Of course the Leader has a kernel of sadness in his green heart, if anyone cared to ask, which nobody ever has. Some days, some nights like this he feels as if his whole heart is made of tears.

But not really.

What he really feels is that deep inside his alien chest there is a bloody red beating human heart. Not green, glowing and alien; but bloody, red, beating and human. He knows it is not true, but he wishes that it were. His whole life he has felt it, the human trapped inside his alien body. When he was a tiny alien boy, he used to shut himself in his quarters and fashion what he thought was a good imitation of human clothing out of his bedding and other odds and ends. With the investment of a great deal of time and effort he had made something like a business suit. Though the pants were really more like a skirt that had to be held tightly from behind or it would fall to the ground; and the jacket was really more of a shawl, but never mind. He would put on his outfit and strut back and forth, pretending to carry a briefcase and to be 'going to work.' Predictably, he had been caught and thoroughly shamed. On more than one occasion.

So the tender young alien had given up his business suit but not his dreams. He had bucked up, worked hard and proved himself to be a model alien, the top of the heap. The Leader. And he had dedicated his life to the service of humans.

He is looking out over the city, over the dark grid of streets below him and the towers of light reaching into the black sky, and he can feel them scanning for him. His crew hates it when he hides. But just for tonight, he is letting them dangle, letting them miss him just a bit. He needs some peace so he can think. He is trying to go back to a moment in his past to see if it can shed any light on his current conundrum. Or maybe he is just going back to it because it is beautiful. The alien sits down on the cold concrete ledge and lets the memory come into his mind and take over his senses once again.

It is 1985 and he is visiting his first real human love for the last time. He takes a second to look around the room, to memorize it. The décor is pure '70s madness – wallpaper with flowers as big as your head, heavy white brocade drapes tied back with braided satin sashes, shag carpet, wrought iron headboard, the works. An orgy of pinks and oranges and gold. It is badly in need of a makeover, but he doesn't know it. He loves it. It is perfect for her. *Her.* She who is lying in bed under a tangle of sheets and frilly bedspread. Missy Marston.

Her hair is dyed a terrible drugstore blue-black and teased into a giant mass. There is make-up on her pillow and an ashtray containing five thousand cigarette butts on her bedside table. (He wishes she wouldn't smoke. Smoking is such a bad idea.) Her bed is filled with things that don't belong there, a collection of items fanning out from her head – a Walkman and headphones, cassette tapes and cases, books, magazines, tissues. She is eighteen years old and about to fly the coop, about to shake off her childhood and become something new, though what that can possibly be, he doesn't know. He has invested three years in this girl, three years of the lives of his full-time crew, and still he doesn't understand very much about her. Like most teenage humans, she is very confusing. She is happy and sad, smart and stupid, belligerent and helpless. But he can no longer stick around to try to figure her out; his efforts are needed elsewhere. Besides which, his crew is becoming impatient.

They are convinced she is fine. They are beginning to wonder why they have invested so much time here, what makes her so different from any other adolescent human. Which, as the Leader knows, is precisely nothing. She is the same as all the other ones.

But to him, none of them seem fine and none of them seem ordinary.

It is a cool spring night and a breeze is coming in through the windows. He has been sitting on the carpet, cross-legged, his cheek resting on the mattress, breathing quietly and watching her sleep. He can smell her skin, her hairspray, her cheap roll-on musk perfume. He can smell stale cigarette smoke and old sneakers. He knows he has to go, that the others are waiting. (Oh, the others, the others! His ragtag group of disciples, his so-called crew. Grumblers and malcontents, all. Such short attention spans! But, what had he expected? He had sought them out and found them, the most unsettled, most disenfranchised of his alien brethren. He had convinced them to turn their green backs on their peaceful, orderly, cultured race and join him in an entirely capricious quest: spying on and meddling with earthlings.

Because he loved them.

Romantically.

For no good reason.

Obviously, this was not how he had sold it to them in the beginning. He described a voyage of discovery, an elite crew living a life of daring and adventure. There would be precision missions, measured interventions – details to follow at a later date, etcetera, – that would reset the course of human history! Their secret operation would, in all likelihood, prevent or at least delay the otherwise certain self-destruction of a beautiful, if misguided race. They would be heroes!

And it would allow him to enter the bedrooms of young earth women and gaze wistfully at their sleeping faces. If only they would just let him be.)

He stands up and looks down at her wondering if she will remember him when he is gone. If she will tell her friends about the strange, recurring dreams she has had that have suddenly stopped. Gingerly, he picks up the book closest to her head. It is a hardcover, dust jacket long gone, cream coloured with a maroon spine. The gold lettering says: **Atwood The Handmaid's Tale.**

He turns the book over in his hand, flips to the title page and sees a handwritten message in black ink: *For Missy – best wishes – Margaret Atwood*. This makes him feel a little bit better; it makes him feel like maybe his subject will be OK after all. Someone else is looking out for her, wishing for her. The Leader closes the book and, holding his breath, places it back beside the sleeping teenager. Best wishes, he thinks. For Missy.

Back in the new millennium, the Leader leaves the scene in his memory, closes the door to that little room again, and stands tall and visible on the ledge. He has a plan in mind, a radical intervention in the human world. He spreads his arms wide and, letting his head fall back, he looks up at the sky. Without looking down, he lets his body fall forward, a slow swan dive. He plummets down ten stories, the wind roaring in his ears, before tucking his knees to his chest and teleporting back to the ship.

Four

The province of mothers

Rose has made up her mind. She has had enough of waiting around for Margaret to call and she has had enough of lying in bed every night and worrying. She has bought a ticket and packed a bag and she is going east to intervene in her daughter's life. She knows that her intervention will be unwelcome. She also knows that unwelcome interventions are the God-given province of wives and mothers everywhere. It is a method she has used with excellent results, many times. Adult humans don't often take advantage of their mothers, but often they can be of use. Often, they are just what the doctor ordered!

Ron and Rose had been watching a television show called *Kink*. It was a documentary series which examined the oddball sexual habits of average Americans. This particular instalment followed the lives of several adult men that liked to dress as infants and be coddled and diapered and suckled by prostitutes dressed as maids or nannies (though the women's outfits and demeanour were, in Rose's opinion, singularly unconvincing). The men had spoken at great length about their motivations for behaving as babies and each one had made the claim that the basis for their desires and their peculiar practices was not, in fact, sexual; it was *emotional*. Rose could well believe it. It didn't seem remotely sexy to her. Plus, there was something about these man-babies that offended her on behalf of mothers everywhere.

Rose understood that, to some extent, everyone wants their mother or the idea of a mother their whole lives. People want comfort and kindness and warmth. What she finds to be an affront, however, is that most adults do not want the *reality* of their mothers. They do not want (or they think they don't want) the meddling, possibly dependent, senior citizens their mothers have become. The ones with opinions and problems and demands. No. When adult life feels too hard and too ugly, people want something like the memory or the fantasy of their young mothers: pretty and indulgent and soft-spoken. We are all man-babies inside sometimes.

Some of us more than others, apparently. Apparently, some of us are babies on the outside, too. Weirdos.

It had been this television show and her musings about it that had convinced Rose to make her move. She felt that Margaret needed her and she, Rose, wanted to know what the hell was going on in her daughter's life. She wanted to see her child's face and she wanted to see where she was living. She also, to be quite honest, fancied a trip. She was feeling a bit cooped up and bored lately. She would not be calling ahead for she knew that she would be rebuffed. Margaret had made it quite clear that a visit was not desired. No matter. Rose had lots of old friends she could stay with if Margaret was away or if she decided to be difficult. She could make arrangements easily enough.

She would also like to have a word with her son-in-law, Brian. Perhaps a word he had never heard her say before. One she has been practicing with him in mind. Her return flight was booked a week hence, so there would be plenty of time for everyone to get a good dose of real mother. Not some tarted-up baby-talking milkmaid. Nope. A dose of real live old-lady she-bear style mother. She could even, for a small fee, reschedule her flight and extend her stay. She was in the mood to speak her mind and it might take a while.

Her husband, it seemed, was also in the mood to speak up. This was a rare and sobering occurrence. Ron had told his wife that her plan was ill-advised, that it would not be productive and that it would end in tears.

"Why do this? Give her a moment to figure things out on her own. She will hate you for it."

"Ron, sweetheart, stop. Every time I talk to her she sounds terrible. She needs my help."

"Do not go see Brian. They are in the middle of a divorce. You will not help and Margaret will not thank you for interfering." Ron said these things knowing full well that Rose would do exactly as she pleased. He did hope to slow her down, to temper her a little.

Rose considered her husband. His face made her smile. She would miss him when she was away. She would miss getting into bed each night and feeling the heat of him, smelling the skin of his shoulder. Almost every night for almost forty years Ron and Rose have climbed into their bed from opposite sides and lain facing each other to cuddle up and review the day. Sometimes they would have sex in a leisurely, conversational kind of way. Sometimes they wouldn't bother. Either way, he would sooner or later roll away from her, onto his own side of the bed and begin to snore. And Rose would lay there and take a long, long time to fall asleep. She would think and plan and, some nights, grumble and fret and get up and pace. She always got a few hours sleep in before morning, though. Most nights her husband was asleep before her and most mornings he was still asleep when she awakened. Rose had grown accustomed to this and, in the end, tried to savour having this time to be alone, unobserved.

A moment to herself was never a bad thing.

And now she would have a week of nights sleeping alone, a week of days to set things right with Margaret. She had faith in the purpose of her journey.

"I won't be stupid, darling, and I won't be gone long. Please don't worry."

Rose planted a loud kiss on her husband's cheek and called for a taxi.

My office is a litter box

THE CONTENTS OF THE ENVELOPE lie in wait on Margaret's kitchen table. She has been avoiding the envelope for weeks now. For all she knows she has missed the workshop on Difference in the Workplace. It has not been raised with her recently and she has been going about her business at work as though the whole ugly business had never happened. She has been careful to be neither friendlier nor cooler to her colleagues than usual. She has concentrated on doing her work perfectly and acting perfectly neutral at all times. Gentle and mild. But the envelope is eating away at her. It has been staring at her from her kitchen table. It winks at her. It begs and cajoles. It whines and wheedles. It wants to be set free!

Finally, one evening, gin mug in hand, Margaret sits down at the table and tears it open and pulls the contents out: a sheaf of papers, a slim volume entitled *The Personality Rainbow*, a spiral-bound exercise book and a small stack of index cards. Margaret doesn't like the look of this one bit. The top sheet is a letter beginning, "Dear participant." The letter informs Margaret that all participants are expected to do some reading and preparation prior to the session on November 5th. (Margaret glances at the calendar, with the sad knowledge that she has not, by some happy accident, missed the course and also that she has limited time to prepare. The workshop is less than a week away.)

The assigned tasks are as follows. *1) Read the book included in this package. 2) Think about how the lessons presented apply to your own life.* Margaret flips through the book and turns it over. A smiling jackass of a woman beams off the back cover at her. Jenny Franco has been helping people get along for more than thirty years! *3) Work through pages 1-12 in your exercise book. Answer honestly and thoroughly. There are no wrong answers!* Margaret groans aloud and turns to the first page of the exercise book. The first question reads: *Think of a metaphor for your workplace (is it a garden? a traffic jam?). How would you describe your role there?*

What about others? How do people work together? Try to stick to your metaphor. Don't worry if it doesn't quite make sense. The object is to get you thinking about the workplace in a new and honest way! Margaret gets up and walks away from the table. She sits on the couch and looks out the window. How will she ever get through this ridiculous thing? She knows she will hate the book. She knows that any honest answer she gives to any question about her office will reveal her putrid heart.

- My office is a litter box and we are all turds.
- My office is a sad parade. A silly, pointless set of motions, performed day after day after day.
- My office is the button factory.
- My office is nothing and I am zero.

Margaret sits staring out the window for some time, thinking nothing, noticing nothing. An hour goes by. She wanders into the bathroom and looks in the mirror and stares. She begins to divide her long, straight hair into sections with a comb and working it into tiny, tight braids. She does this very, very slowly. She takes each section between her thumb and index finger. She slides them down the section of hair from her scalp to the ends. She does this over and over again. At least twenty slow strokes. Then she divides it into three smaller sections and painstakingly and rhythmically winds them together into braids.

The aliens look on with concern. What is she doing? Why is she doing it so slowly and so carefully?

Margaret is thinking nothing and looking at nothing and slowly working her hair into the smallest, tightest braids possible. She is not doing a very good job. The braids are not the same size, are not tidy and even. She has nothing to secure the ends of the braids with, so some are coming undone. She can't see the braids at the back of her head, so these are turning out to be extra-crazy. Finally, she finishes her task and takes a hard look at the result.

She stares at herself and her self stares back. What do we have before us? Margaret tries to assess herself dispassionately. She is still wearing her work clothes – a red pullover (faded and too tight) and a grey jacket. There is a crusty smudge of toothpaste in the middle of her chest, on what she thinks of as the *prow* of her bosom, and the collar of her jacket is turned up on one side. The jacket is wrinkled at the elbows. Margaret leans in so that her face is about three inches from the glass. Her glasses are filthy. She removes them. She presses a thumb over the creases between her eyes. She runs her hands down the side of her face and pulls her cheeks tight until her nostrils flare and her lips flatten out against her teeth. She lets her hands fall to her side and looks at her crazy, witchy hair. Margaret sighs, sticks her tongue out at her reflection, gives it the finger and turns away.

Back at the kitchen table, Margaret flips through the exercise book to find out what the recipe cards are for and after a time finds her answer. *Question ten: Write your name on the back of all six of the cards provided. Now think of six people that you love. On the other side of each card, write down how each of these people is different from you.* Refilling her cup with gin, Margaret decides to make a card for six people she hates and enumerate why. This is what she writes down:

1. Brian: Number one on the shit-list. Top of the charts. Where to begin? I hate you for wasting my life, for stealing my youth. For being so disgusting, so completely unworthy of love and yet attracting every brainless woman who has ever had the misfortune of meeting you. For being a shameless, guiltless monster instead of a human husband.

    I curse you.

    I hope every part of you erupts with hideous boils and warts. I hope you start giving off a terrible, indomitable odour. I hope it surrounds you in a foul cloud. I hope it precedes you when you walk into a room, announcing your arrival, and I hope it lingers behind you when you leave.

So people can tell.

I hope you begin to look and smell like what you are: a piece of shit.

A shit monster.

(Margaret's printing is getting smaller and smaller and she has run out of space on Brian's card, so decides to leave it there. Who's next? Ah, yes.)

2. Marie: For telling on me. And for being so exhaustingly young and pretty and good. You make me vomit.

(Good. Concise. She is getting the hang of it now.)

3. My mother: For not ever letting me be.
4. Sandie (and so many others): For not letting my husband be.
5. Lenny: For lecturing me. For making me suffer through this humiliating exercise. For not giving me my due. For not giving me some kind of fucking medal for enduring my meaningless job for so many years. For looking like a tit with that hair. Seriously. How old are you anyway?
6. My father: For not mattering more.

She feels a bit guilty about that last one. Who could hate her father? Who would bother? She is starting to feel sad and tired and sick of herself.

Margaret flips through the cards and marvels at how little any of it matters. Boring. She regrets having ruined the cards and she regrets letting her feelings see the light of day. Written down on cards, how foolish they seem, how embarrassing. She folds each one four times and puts them in the trash under the sink. She looks at the clock on the stove. The time is 8:00 p.m. How can time move so slowly? How can it crawl this way? What is she supposed to do in this place night after night after night after night?

Margaret makes a decision. She will go out. She will shove a stupid hat over her stupid hair, brush her teeth and walk out the door.

Trick or treat

WELL, THE ALIENS COULDN'T be more surprised! They are certain that Margaret hasn't been out in the evening since moving into her apartment. Absolutely certain. This throws a wrench in the works, indeed! Working on the assumption that Margaret would get drunk alone and go to bed early as usual, the aliens had planned a visit for the Leader around 10:00 p.m.

It had seemed perfectly reasonable.

Foolproof, even.

And he is not the only one planning a visit. There is also Margaret's mother, already launched into the air and soon to descend. Now what? The aliens gather around the screen, elbowing each other out of the way so they can follow Margaret's slow, slightly weaving meander down the street to the bus stop.

Margaret sits on the cold bench at the bus stop, heart pounding. Now that she is out of the house, she feels nervous. She scans the dark, tree-lined street for drunks and crazies. 'Perps.' The thought of this word she has learned from cop shows makes her laugh to herself. Silly word! How could anyone feel tough saying that word? 'Perps.' She slouches down on the bench and tilts her head back and looks at the sky. There is a bright full moon and Margaret can see the shadow of clouds around its edges. She begins to relax a little and to feel like maybe she could fall asleep right here on this bench if it weren't so frigging cold.

The aliens don't know what Margaret is thinking, taking the bus at this hour on a weeknight. The schedule is terrible. She could be sitting on that bench for an hour before any bus comes! They are becoming anxious watching her. What if she does fall asleep? What if she gets attacked on the street? What if she stays out late and misses her mother's arrival? Where on earth does she think she's going anyway?

Yes, the aliens have been watching Rose, too. They have watched the arc of her plane, rising from the ground, up above the clouds and hurtling toward Margaret. From the light of the West into the moonlit sky of the East. Trailing fumes behind it, tearing through the fabric of the air, passing over cities and towns and lakes and rivers and fields and trees. The mother flying to the rescue of the daughter. If only Margaret would wait. If only she would just stay home and wait!

Margaret sits up straight and squints down the street, looking for some sign of a bus. Nothing. She looks the other way and is startled to see the Leader sitting on the bench beside her. Confused, she scans the street again and is amazed to notice glowing pumpkins on every porch. Halloween! She had not made the connection. She had lost track of the days, somehow become disconnected with the normal human timetable. Straggling groups of kids wander by, most of them adult-sized and half-heartedly costumed. The little ones have already been and gone. Burned out and faded away, asleep in piles of Snickers bars and Rockets candies, tucked away in their houses. Drooling chocolate and lipstick onto their pillow cases. Margaret turns once more to her companion on the bench.

The Leader had barely recognized Margaret with that hat. A black and white striped knit hat, shaped like a dented smokestack. A most unlikely hat! But, in the end, he knew his quarry. He knew her by her smell and her walk and by the shape of her pretty mouth. And she had not really ventured very far from home in the end, thank goodness.

The Leader looks at Margaret and she looks back. He straightens her hat and runs his hand down the side of her face. Ever so slowly, he leans in and puts his cheek against hers. He breathes quietly into her ear. Margaret closes her eyes and leans into him as he plants a papery warm kiss on her cheek.

Jack-o-lanterns are extinguished and doors slam shut. Porch lights go out and the bus thunders past, a plume of dried leaves in its wake.

There is a ball of pink-orange light beside the full moon that pulses twice and fades away as the Leader helps Margaret off the bench and walks her home.

Rose's secrets

THE FLIGHT ATTENDANT IS looking at Rose expectantly and Rose, for her part, cannot imagine what it is that the girl wants. Obviously, she has been sleeping. The flight attendant repeats the words she has been repeating in precisely the same manner to each passenger in each seat, from the front of the plane to the very back row, where Rose sits, befuddled.

"Cookie? Beverage?" Rose only smiles serenely. For some reason, she finds the question very, very funny. The stewardess is stumped for a moment, a scowl makes a brief appearance on her perfectly made-up face before she turns brightly to the man sitting next to Rose. "Cookie? Beverage?"

Rose snorts and looks out the window. A field of cloud stretches below her, as the plane glides through the sparkling sky above. How childish she can be sometimes and how she loves to be childish! Ridiculous in a woman her age. She finds it bubbles up, irresistibly and frequently: this desire to rattle people, to act in ways they don't expect for no good reason. It makes her laugh. Often out loud and at the wrong times. Deliberately misbehaving in this way is one of Rose's most closely guarded secrets. She would deny it until death.

And it is not her only secret. She has two others.

Rose has long believed that having at least one appalling secret that no one could guess is good for the soul. She also thinks that it is good for a marriage to keep at least a small part of yourself in reserve. It puts a sparkle in your eye and gives you an air of mystery.

Rose's first secret is that she has, at the age of sixty-five, started smoking pot with her girlfriend, Marianne Dalrymple. Marianne, known by most as 'Doll,' is ten years Rose's junior and lives right across the street. She is recently divorced and revelling in her new single lifestyle. She and Rose have spent many an afternoon at Doll's kitchen table, sharing a joint and laughing their silly heads off. They don't do this every day, not even every week. It has to be plotted and planned and carried out like a secret mission. Ideally, it should be on a day when Ron has a scheduled appointment, so that Rose can float back across the road, gargle with mouthwash, douse herself with perfume and arrange her face into a serious expression by the time he gets home.

Occasionally, too, Rose has procured some pot from Doll to smoke on her own. She especially likes to get high and then go grocery shopping or do laundry. This is good for a couple of reasons. Number one is the spy factor. Nobody would expect a sixty-five-year-old woman doing her groceries to be stoned. It is outrageous to imagine! She has found that in the disguise that is her normal self, she can walk down the street smoking pot in full view and not ever provoke a second glance. It is as though she is invisible. Secondly, both groceries and laundry are slow, comforting, orderly tasks that can irritate the life out of a person if one is too alert and fidgety. But, groceries and laundry under the influence of marijuana can be the gentlest and dreamiest of games. Easy does it ... eight perfectly folded washcloths ... ten carefully selected peaches.

Rose's other entirely concealed spy secret is that she likes (yes, at her age) to masturbate with a vibrator. Hidden at the back of her top dresser drawer, wrapped in a sock, is a quiet, rechargeable, egg-shaped machine. It is smooth and black and had cost her an astonishing $89.95. Buying it was one of the most thrilling secret missions of her life so far! She walked into a lovely and quiet store for women only and chatted with the clerk as though it were not the most embarrassing thing in the whole world. She could barely hear her own voice for the rushing of blood in her ears. She had felt faint. But she smiled and chatted and walked out of that store with her little package tucked in her purse. She really had felt like a spy! Mission accomplished! I have the microfilm!

Rose rests her forehead against the edge of the window and stares out at the clouds. They fan out as far as the eye can see like a great expanse of shearling wool. It reminds Rose of a sheepskin coat she had in the '70s. It had a sleek cut, with a tie at the waist and a massive, puffy collar. Foxy-looking and oppressively hot. You couldn't wear that thing indoors for a minute without drenching your clothes in sweat. She wonders where that coat is now and if it would fit around her. Her middle is larger than it used to be. Infuriating slow outward creep of the belly!

Suddenly, the plane lurches and Rose smacks her head painfully against the moulded plastic window frame. "Shit!" She presses her hand against her head, smiles distractedly at the startled young man beside her, and tries to think of something that will make the pain go away and prevent the bruise she can feel gathering strength beneath her skin. She rummages around in her purse and finds a Wet-Nap which she unwraps, unfolds and presses against her forehead. It is cool and smells like lemons. She sighs and leans back into her seat and hopes for the best. Soon, she is asleep again. The Wet-Nap takes on the heat of her head, slowly leeches its moisture into the air of the cabin and when it is entirely dried out, flutters into Rose's lap.

Meanwhile, a small red and black and purple bruise in the shape of a crescent moon blossoms into being, just above her left eyebrow.

And speaking of spies

THE LEADER CLOSES THE FRONT door of the apartment building behind Margaret and takes a deep, long breath. Through the glass, he watches her make her unsteady way up the stairs and out of sight.

In case you have been wondering if he knows the difference, of course he does. He knows that this Margaret Atwood did not write that book lying in young Missy Marston's bed. That book! It had given him nightmares for weeks. He would wake up hiccupping and sobbing. A vision so dark, so cold. Terrifying to contemplate. Here was a stern warning from a real prophet about the death of all the things that made humans good: art and invention, love and tenderness, silliness and jokes. That magic potion that runs through human veins. All gone.

Or almost gone.

It couldn't be killed. Not ever. Margaret E. Atwood knew this. There was a glimmer on every page of that book. Not just in the story or the characters, their bitter, stubborn, spindly hopes pushing up like weeds through concrete, but in the beauty of the words. The Leader can hardly believe it. He struggles to understand how it can be done. The words so precisely arranged to illuminate every moment, ugly or not, with human magic. Like another story beneath the story, written in invisible ink.

Cannot be killed.

The Leader knew it, too. But it wouldn't do to take a chance. Painful as it was, the Leader was glad he had read that sobering Tale. It had given him focus; it had given his shenanigans a higher purpose.

He had tried to give it up, his interference with human goings-on. His lovelorn fantasies, his trans-specied tendencies. He had tried to turn his attention to a normal, healthy alien life. He had tried to respect his heritage. But he couldn't stop watching them, spying. He couldn't stop meddling. Not just because it was fun. But also because he might be able to help. Just a little bit.

Yes, he was well aware of the many differences between Margaret the Checker and Margaret the Prophet. He knew Margaret had not written that book. Or any other book. But her name had been a sign.

He had started with a number of candidates, a selection of earthlings in various locations around the globe. Beautiful earth women, each with her own talents, her own compelling story. But he always came back to her. He had waited so long for some hint, some excuse to assemble his crew and descend again to earth. Then, one day, he had seen her sign her name on a credit card slip at the liquor store, her hair falling across her face, her eyes welling with tears, and he had followed her home. Margaret H. Atwood.

The Universe had spoken.

She would be the One.

He sits down on the cold concrete steps and stares down the street. How beautiful it is. The shimmering streetlights haloed against the black, black sky. The little boxes of houses. The flashing, blue light that makes every front window into a kind of television. He could watch for hours, just absorbing the beauty of earthly life, dreaming of inhabiting a human body. Any imperfect human body.

It is time to make his way back, though. He has already been here too long. Someone will notice that he is a little too tall, that his proportions are a little wrong. Someone might get close enough to see that his costume is not a costume at all. And he would rather not see the look in their eyes. The terror and disgust.

It hurts his feelings.

One story up

MARGARET IS LYING ON HER BACK on the carpeted floor of the landing. She is staring at the shell-shaped glass light fixture above and letting her eyes go in and out of focus. There is a glow around the light that fattens up nicely if she lets her eyes go fuzzy. She is not completely insane: she is around a corner and out of view, half-listening for a tread on the stairs. She is confident that she could spring up and trot up the remaining stairs to her apartment if the need arose. She is just taking a moment. She is delaying her arrival. And she is thinking about something bright and beautiful that she remembers from childhood.

When she was a girl, her parents had rented a cottage for a couple of weeks every summer. She had always resisted going because it was lonely and boring there. Often there were no other kids her age on the lake. There was no television. Her parents got on her nerves. She always had to be coaxed and cajoled. Though once there, she had loved it. She had revelled in the cool air of the forest, the bright-hot sun and the absolute summer quiet, so different from the city block they lived on, so different from the din of school.

Lying on her back on the itchy carpet, Margaret remembers diving off the end of the dock and swimming hard and straight, away from the cottage, to the middle of the lake. She would lie on her back with her ears submerged and stare at the giant dome of blue sky, running her fingers slowly back and forth through the rippling water. She remembers floating there and taking note of the things you could hear if you were perfectly still, with your ears underwater like that. You could hear your own breathing, your own voice if you spoke or sang or hummed. Occasionally, you could hear the sound of a boat engine, made strangely high-pitched under the water. What you couldn't hear, ever, were these: the hundred or so spiders working away underneath the docks, some of them the size of the palm of your hand; the thousands of bass, slick and brown-and-green speckled on top and white speckled from below, making their way through the grassy weeds at the bottom of the lake; the skittering water beetles on the surface of the lake; the few water snakes sliding through the water like ribbons. You could not hear the one giant snapping turtle that occasionally appeared near the shore and terrified children, the turtle that was surely lurking somewhere nearby your splayed, suspended, tender white self.

And one story above that

ONE STORY ABOVE MARGARET, Rose is having a summer memory of her own. She is seated atop her suitcase in the hallway outside of Margaret's door, wondering where the hell she might be and when she might be back. Surely, Rose had known that this was a possibility. Everyone knows that if you choose to arrive unannounced there may be no one there to greet you and it will be your own damned fault. This knowledge though does not prevent Rose from feeling vaguely annoyed with Margaret. She rises above it, though. She zones out and thinks about summertime.

A few summers back, Rose and Ron had spent a week at a small resort on a lake. This lake was nowhere near as lovely as the lake of Margaret's childhood. In fact, Rose doubted that it was a lake at all. It was shallow and perfectly round, like the water-filled impression of a giant flying saucer; it was as though the Lord had tried a shallow spoonful of this earth and had found it to be not quite to his taste. The bottom of the lake was loamy and fine and sent up dense grey clouds as Rose waded tentatively up to her knees on their first day at the resort. She suspected that the lake bed was composed largely of the droppings of the numerous seagulls that bobbed on the surface of the water and wheeled madly in the sky above. Rose had decided that perhaps the best – and safest – way to enjoy this particular lake was from a lounge chair on the beach.

From her perch on the beach Rose had been able to observe the vacationers with which she and Ron were sharing the place for the week. It appeared to be mostly book-toting old folks like themselves and young families attempting to keep their children amused. Rose was particularly charmed by one of the regulars at the beach, a little girl around the age of eight. The girl had two dishwater-brown braids and a blunt, freckled nose. She seemed to dress her skinny-limbed, pot-bellied form exclusively in a striped, one-piece bathing suit. She was prone to loud, barking laughter and to running at top speed. She seemed to Rose an adventurer, a trailblazer of a girl.

One day Rose sat in her chair and watched the girl swim out to the middle of the lake to the water trampoline. This contraption, much touted in the brochure for the resort, was a giant half-inflated inner tube (encrusted with seagull shit) with a limp piece of rubber spanning its top. The girl hoisted herself out of the water, made her way to the centre of the wobbly surface of the trampoline and started bouncing like a lunatic. Higher and higher, water spraying from her hair, a crazy grin on her face. At the apex of every jump, her heels rebounded off her firm little buttocks. To her friend on the beach, the girl shouted, "Oh my God! This is *so wickedly awesome*!"

Rose couldn't help smiling. Personally, she could not imagine anything less wickedly awesome than the so-called water-trampoline, but she loved the unmitigated joy of the girl, the unbridled exuberance. Later the same day, she had overheard the girl talking to her mother. She was refusing to go shopping in the nearby town on the basis that it was "boring and stupid." Clearly, she was a young woman of strong opinions.

Rose often thought of the girl and her strong opinions. It seemed that, in those two short phrases, the girl had aptly described the pendulum swing of daily experience – the two tails of the continuum: on one end, wickedly awesome; at the other, boring and stupid.

Perched here, as she is, on top of her suitcase, in the hallway of her daughter's apartment building, tired from her trip, thirsty and with a splitting headache, Rose is edging ever so slightly past the boring and stupid mark and heading toward all-out vexation. She closes her eyes and leans her head back against the wall. She wishes she could skip the predictable confrontation with Margaret that is before her and slide straight into bed, any bed at all, and sleep.

The turtle

THIS IS WHAT THE TURTLE says: "Margaret, really."

Margaret stares into the small-eyed, striped face of the turtle that is standing on her chest and staring into her eyes. She is aware that the turtle is somehow not a turtle, but someone she has known before, someone with good intentions. She is also aware that she is lying on the floor of the landing of her apartment building and that this is probably a very bad idea. She imagines, though, that the turtle is here for a reason and that it must have something important to tell her. The turtle closes one eye and then the other and sighs a quiet, seaweed-scented sigh.

"Margaret, really. You need to get up off the floor and get upstairs. This is no place to lie down."

To Margaret this seems obvious. However, the weight of the turtle on her chest, whose shell is the size of a dinner plate, makes it impossible for her to take its good advice. There must be more. The fishy green smell of lake water is overwhelming. Moisture from the cool, leathery belly of the turtle is slowly soaking the front of her sweater. It is starting to itch. The turtle stretches its wrinkled neck and clears its throat.

"Margaret, Margaret, Margaret. Let me tell you something: there are five million things you could be doing instead of lying here on your back. Five million things that are better. Picking lint off a sweater would be better. Just standing up would be better. You are on a bad path, Margaret. This is the path that leads to muttering and wetting your pants in the grocery store, to picking fights with strangers in the street. You need to get up. You need to gather your strength and be a person. A *grown person*, for Christ's sake."

Margaret stares at the turtle and is not sure whether to be affronted by its presumption or to be touched that it gives a damn. She raises a heavy hand slowly up off of the floor to place it gingerly on the turtle's shell and finds that it rests instead on the back of the sweaty hand of her own real-life mother. Shifting her gaze upward, she confronts Rose's glaring countenance atop her wrinkled turtle neck. The wise turtle is her mother. Fuck.

Margaret follows her mother up the stairs like the child she is – and she is not a very smart one either. Her hair is outrageous; there is lint and dirt clinging to her back, possibly drool on the front of her sweater. Lower, anyone? She knows that the situation with her mother can only get worse, so she decides to stay quiet and take orders for the moment.

Once in the apartment, Rose bustles around in a rage. She washes dishes, wipes counters, makes beds, lecturing all the while. She talks and talks and talks until she is sick of the sound of her own voice. Margaret makes no attempt to respond. Finally, Rose sends Margaret to bed. She is too vexed, too wound up to go to bed herself.

With her grown wreck of a daughter snoring in the other room, Rose leans against the windowsill and strains to look up at the sky above the tops of buildings. The night is clear and there are glittering stars and she is so tired that her bones feel hollow.

The Leader, surrounded by his adoring minions, in their orange-pink ship in the sky, stares at the screen before him and quietly thanks Rose. He knows his place, wise turtle that he is. He knows there is only so much one alien can do for someone like Margaret.

You can get off now

"Mom, what happened to your head?" Margaret notes the dark purple bruise on Rose's forehead.

"I'll ask the questions around here, if you don't mind."

"Don't be like that. It's just worrisome, that's all."

"Ha! That's rich."

Mom, please don't be here if you are just going to be angry at me for being pathetic. It doesn't help."

"Who says I want to help?"

"Mom. Please. I am begging you." Margaret's head is pounding.

Rose gets up from the kitchen table and walks over to where Margaret is sitting on the couch. To Margaret's great surprise, she lowers her big, soft self onto her lap. The weight is crushing. And hot. "How does that feel Margaret?"

"What? It feels terrible! Get off!"

Rose leans in close to Margaret's face: "This is how I feel Margaret. Like a grown woman is sitting on my lap. I cannot take care of you anymore. Do you hear me? You have to take care of yourself."

"Then go home!" Margaret cannot believe the idiocy of this exchange. It makes her more tired. She lets her head fall forward onto the fleshy shoulder of her mother. "I have to go to work now, Mom. Thank you for coming here. Thank you for trying to help me. I don't want you to go, I didn't mean it. I do want you to get off now, though."

At this Rose starts to cry. It is all so silly, so incredibly frustrating. Why is it that children, throughout their whole lives, are most difficult to help when they most need help? Why, at these precise moments, are they so infuriating, so unsympathetic? Is it some twisted function of nature? What use could it possibly be? Why can she, Rose, never ever behave in the way she knows she should in these situations? She should be calming. She should talk sense. Sitting on her: a fantastic idea. How humiliating it all is. How old she feels. Rose hauls herself off her daughter, wipes her tears away, and ambles toward the guest room to unpack.

"Are you going to be alright, Mom?"

"Sorry I sat on you."

"It's OK. A bit weird, though. A bit *dramatic*."

"Don't start. I'll make us something nice for dinner tonight and we can both pretend we're sane."

"See you later, Mom."

Margaret takes her cue and hurries out the door. She gallops down the stairs and out the front door. The air outside is cool and fresh. She stands on the sidewalk in the sunlight and breathes. Then she leans forward with her hands on her knees like a runner just past the finish line. She wonders, fleetingly, if there is somewhere she can possibly go this morning that is not her office and is not her apartment.

She wishes she had another apartment.

Now that this one is contaminated.

Delivery man

MARGARET IS TRYING TO WORK. She stares at the document and her eyes go out of focus, the text blurs. She tries looking out the window for a moment and then back to the page. The text co-operates, becomes crisp and clean and legible again. She reads the words and finds they do not take on any meaning. They are just syllables, sounds that bounce around inside her head and transmit no messages. Has it finally happened? Has she finally been bored senseless? Laughter erupts on the other side of her cubicle wall in a sudden, high-pitched yelp, making her jump in her seat, her pen dropping from her hand. There is the murmuring of voices and she freezes, staring at the wall, trying to make out what is being said. Then, before her heartbeat has returned to normal, she is startled again by the sound of rustling paper directly behind her head. She spins around in her chair to see Marie standing there.

"What?" Jesus, she is surrounded. Sweat is soaking her shirt under her arms. Why is it always so hot in here? She tugs at the collar of her shirt, feeling colour flush her cheeks, sweat beading at her hairline. "Sorry, Marie. What is it?"

"Lenny asked me to give you these." Marie's arms are stretched out straight in front of her like a sleepwalker, a sheaf of papers in her hands. Her head is turned ninety degrees to the right, avoiding Margaret's gaze completely. If she could turn it all the way around, exorcist-style, Margaret is pretty sure she would do it.

"Thanks." Margaret grabs the papers a little more forcefully than she intended.

"They're due tomorrow." Is what Margaret thinks she hears from the back of Marie's head as she walks away.

"Fine," says Margaret. "*Christ,*" she whispers.

Loud throat clearing from the hallway.

Snickers from the next office.

Margaret closes her eyes and silently calls uncle. She throws the papers on top of the pile that is already there and decides it is time for lunch.

Out another door, onto another sidewalk, she is drinking fresh air as though it were water, as though she were only allowed to breathe once a day and then only for precisely one hour. She is still reeling from the fact that her mother has actually visited, has come all this way, is likely in her apartment going through her drawers right now.

At the park, Margaret takes a bench as far away from any other occupied bench as possible and works her way through her lunch, which is her usual schoolgirl special of sandwich, apple, juice box, cookies and cheese. A cool, damp breeze lifts off the river behind her as she chews. A pigeon edges skittishly toward her shoe and she kicks at it. The thought of pigeons disgusts her. She imagines that beneath the feathers, their scabby skin is crawling with disease. Likely, they are covered with lice and maggots and some kind of special horrible bird-grease. She stomps her foot hard on the pavement. The pigeon takes a couple of steps backward, turns and stalks away.

Margaret wants to think about the night before. She wants to carefully think through the sequence of events, because part of the evening seems to be missing. She remembers leaving the apartment, swaying drunkenly to the bus stop. With painful accuracy, she remembers being hustled off the landing and up the stairs by her mother. But the time between is harder. It is, in fact, gone. If she pulls her mind back to the bench at the bus stop, she has sort of an impression, if not exactly a memory. It is a dreamy, nostalgic feeling. A school-dance-summer-camp kind of feeling. If she slows down the tape of her mind and forces herself up off the bench at the bus stop and down the street toward her home, she can feel the ghost of an arm around her waist. If, with her will, she moves her body up the stairs of her building and looks back at the front door, she can see a shape through the glass.

There is something about this shape in the window that pulls at her. She wants to go to it, away from the tangled, claustrophobic mess that is her life. Away from her mother and the hornets' nest that is her office, away from the ugly fissure that is her divorce.

Margaret knows this figure, knows that it has featured in her dreams of late. She feels that if she closes her eyes long enough, if she lets her mind wander, she will see it clearly. She will dream it back into her head and she will have some comfort. She will be delivered.

    Margaret squints up at the sky and feels the cool breeze whistle past her ears. She is cold in her light coat. Her hands are dry and chapped and freezing. She squeezes the remains of her lunch through the paper bag she brought it in. She shapes it into a ball and sends it in an arc into the wire garbage can at the end of the bench. She stands up straight and prepares her head for re-entry into the office, into her sticky cell in the vibrating hive.

The vessel

LYING IN BED THAT NIGHT, Margaret stares at the ceiling. She flips to her side, lifts her head to smooth the creases out of her pillow, puts her head back down. She lifts her head again, flips the pillow over, hoping the other side will be cooler and somehow better, to no avail. She turns to her stomach, to her other side, to her back again, in rapid succession. She kicks at the covers, which she feels are confining her somehow, are *pinning her to the bed*. She throws them off entirely. She puts them on again, plucking at them like a demented, nesting bird. She brings the clock close to her face: 2:00 a.m.

She frets about not sleeping, which causes her not to sleep.

She cannot stop thinking about that asinine workshop. Every line she has read from the assigned book – though admittedly she has read very few – runs through her mind with accompanying scathing commentary. She thinks that this kind of so-called self-discovery workshop can only really work (if they ever really work) for people who normally sail along the surfaces of their lives and never take a good hard look at themselves.

Clearly they are not for people in crisis, not for people whose every flaw, whose every misbegotten dream waggles before them like so many funhouse skeletons every minute of every day. These people will not sportingly *workshop* their feelings in polite company and be mildly surprised by what they discover; these people, her tribe, will stay stonily silent, or speak, then weep, then flee the room.

She is filled with dread. What horrible things will leak out of her in front of strangers?

Margaret gets out of bed and pads quietly down the hallway, past the guest room where her mother is sleeping flat on her back, snoring with the door wide open. She slips into the bathroom and eases the door shut. She does not turn on the light, as she knows that doing so will render her blind for her return trip down the hallway.

Moonlight filters in through the small window by the toilet. With resignation, she realizes that she does not, in fact, have to pee, that this is a false alarm, an insomniac red herring. Margaret sits on the edge of the tub and looks up at the window. She imagines that the rectangle of blue light is a blank page, that her mind is a blank page. She realizes that she has been breathing quickly and attempts to slow herself down. She tries to breathe as though she were pretending to sleep. Heavily, slowly, breathing in and out. The bathroom in the middle of the night seems to her the most beautiful place on earth. It is so cool and quiet and everything is blue-grey from the moonlight – the tub, the toilet, the counter. The small room and everything in it looks as though it were made of smooth stone. It feels sealed. It feels as private and serene and holy as a tomb.

She could stay here forever.

No, she is not surprised to feel the heat of the Leader's thigh against hers. She had somehow been hoping that he would make an appearance. She turns to get a good look at him, sitting there beside her on the edge of the tub. His face is very close to hers. His skin is smooth and not scaly, though it shines in a most peculiar way. She notices that what she had previously mistaken for giant, black eyes are really glasses of some kind. She can see his real eyes behind the lenses and they are, in a way, not very different from her own eyes, and Margaret thinks, *Please, remember this. Please, let this come to me when I am sad and desperate. I need to remember*.

The alien is holding something the size and shape of a shoebox. He looks from the box to Margaret and says, silently, *Don't be afraid. You can do it. Have faith.*

Margaret reaches over, deliberately and slowly brushing her bare arm against the alien's bare chest as she does, and removes the lid of the box. There is a loud, deep humming in her ears. The box is packed with honeycomb and teeming with bees. *Have faith*, says the alien and softly kisses her cheek. She presses her ear against the side of his face and breathes in the clean, sweet smell of his skin. As they part, Margaret slowly lowers her hand into the box in his lap and dislodges a waxy wedge of honeycomb. She lifts it up and honey drips down her arm. Bees are crawling down her arm, into her armpit, under her t-shirt, into her hair. A tingling heat follows them and she begins to laugh and laugh.

The Leader lets Margaret laugh for as long as she needs to, for as long as it takes for her to fall asleep, leaning heavily against him. Then he hoists her up over his shoulder, firefighter style. He carries her down the hallway, leaving a trail of golden space honey on the floor behind them. He stops outside the open door of Rose's room and looks at her lying there, arms spread wide, mouth hanging open. Now, here is the sleep of a contented human mind. No intervention required here in the guest room. She is doing just fine.

Unlike this one. The Leader pats Margaret fondly on the behind and carries her back to her room, where he swings her onto the bed.

To him, she weighs nothing.

She is a balloon.

A perfect empty vessel.

Five

The white board

IN HER DETERMINATION to be useful in a crisis, Rose has devised a system. She has purchased a whiteboard, which is now nailed to Margaret's living room wall, and a set of erasable markers. On this board, in her barely legible hand, is a list of things that must be accomplished before she will fly back to her home and her husband and her very pleasant life. As she has explained to Margaret, they will work through this list together, as a team. The list has come into being by way of a tearful, gin-fuelled and seemingly endless conference between the two women and reads thus:

1. Prepare for workshop
2. Survive workshop
3. Take action to divorce your husband – don't be passive
4. Reclaim your dignity at the office or quit your job
5. Get a haircut (this thrown in by Rose to make sure there was an easy one)
6. Be less boring

After this the list becomes less sensible, less legible. Unnumbered items trail down the balance of the board, including be less spiteful, be less drunk and express yourself through violence, following which are a number of dots, dashes and smudges.

On the whole, Rose is pleased with this list. She thinks it is a good framework. And though Margaret has complained bitterly about it, she has found a strange comfort in the list. It is an admission of defeat that has allowed her to stop raging against things – it is the psychic equivalent of going limp in an auto accident to minimize physical harm. The list had been looming there anyway, even before it was written down. Now that it is written on the wall, she can give it the finger as she passes by and, with any luck, cross the odd thing off.

With only two days left before her seminar, Margaret is dutifully spending her evenings preparing. This has had two much-desired side effects: it blocks other thoughts (such as those concerning her co-workers or Brian) and it blocks conversation with Rose. Margaret has read or at least scanned the idiot book and has divined the theme, which appears to be something along the lines of: be nice or be quiet. She has given due consideration to her workplace metaphor and her role within it and after considerable struggle has come up with something that she believes is both accurate and possible for her to say aloud among strangers. It has been interesting to her that every option she has considered, including the one she will use, is so trite as to be absurd. My office is a sandwich, a machine, a garden, etc. Is it because it is a stupid exercise or is it because, through sheer underuse, her thinking has really become so boiled down and limited? She needs to stimulate her brain, start reading the paper again, watching the news. Perhaps it is because her office really is meaningless. It really is a sandwich.

While Margaret toils away at the kitchen table, Rose enters the bathroom and locks the door behind her. She opens the small window and lights a joint. The sky outside is dark blue. She sits on the countertop, her back pressed against the mirror and lets her legs dangle over the edge. She feels the familiar, warm buzz settling over her brain and smiles to herself. Secretly, she is making her own list. She flicks ash into the sink, turns on the faucet to wash it away.

Margaret can smell the pot smoke that has filled the bathroom and is now leaking out under the door into the hallway and suffusing her shoebox-sized apartment with its marshy odour. And of course it is not the first time. Margaret puts her pen down and glares in the direction of the bathroom.

"*Mom!*"

Something clatters to the floor inside the bathroom. "Mom?"

There is a thump, a flush, running water. Throat clearing.

"Yes?" Rose emerges, squinting.

"Are you kidding me?"

"What?"

"Are you going to pretend that you were not just smoking pot in the bathroom? Really?"

"I don't think so," says Rose, grinning. "I don't think it will get me very far. *Sorry, Mom.*"

"Very funny."

"I thought so." That Rose finds her own joke very funny is clear: she is laughing so hard she can barely catch her breath. Tears are streaming down her face. She is having much more fun on this trip than she thought she would. And she has a feeling it will only get better. Margaret rolls her eyes and waves her toward the bedroom. "Goodnight, Mom. Crazy old stoner. Jesus Christ."

Smiling Rose drifts down the hallway, throws a half-hearted wave over her shoulder, "Goodnight, sweetie."

A surprise for Brian

BRIAN IS SEATED AT HIS DESK, talking on the phone, when he looks up to see his mother-in-law, of all people, standing in the doorway of his office. She smiles and winks; he turns his back to her and finishes his call. He takes his time, winds the conversation slowly down, so that in parallel he can think about what to say to her. Something that will not hamper, and that might possibly advance, his plans. Rose waits patiently by the door. She does not want to interfere with Brian's business. She does not, as he may fear, want to make a scene. She simply wants to give him some important information. And she can wait. She knows how to enjoy a moment.

Half-listening to Brian's patter, she wonders if she knew from the beginning how deeply shitty he was. She thinks back to their first meeting when Margaret was still in school, when Brian was hauled into their family home to have a meal, to be approved by the parents. He had been so sloppy then, had seemed so unlikely to become what he is now: a gleaming, perfectly-buffed professional. There had been something charming about him. His smile was nice. He had always been bossy, though, and always unaccountably pleased with himself. Rose supposes that she had found Brian irritating and somehow suspect from the beginning.

This is true.

There had been something else, though, something worse. As clever and funny and seemingly gallant as he could be at times, Rose had always suspected that there was a cold-bloodedness about Brian. She sensed that, if circumstances demanded it, he would, with no small degree of relish, kill you and eat you. There was this and there was the fact that, at any given moment, if you followed the trajectory of Brian's gaze, you would find the swaying behind of a beautiful girl that just happened to be walking by.

"Rose! This is unexpected."

"How are you, Brian?"

"Just fine, thanks. Busy at the moment, though."

"All is well? Things humming along as usual?"

"I suppose. Is there something you wanted, Rose? It's good to see you, as always, you're looking well, but I really do have a full schedule today."

"I know, I know, I won't stay. I just wanted to let you know that I am in town and that Margaret and I have hired Bob Sherman to represent her in the divorce. We were so pleased that he agreed! Now I know that you and Bob are well-acquainted. So, with any luck, we can wrap things up quickly. Alright, I'll get out of your hair now. I'm sure we'll be seeing each other again soon!"

It can only be described as glee, the feeling that Rose has in her heart as she turns to leave Brian's office. Smug little bastard! She smiles at every person she sees as she swaggers through the offices and onto the elevator.

What a wonderful feeling to give someone a surprise!

The colour blank

Brian watches Rose's back as she strides out of his office. He leans forward so he can see her walk out, past reception and out the door to the elevators. Then he reaches for the phone and dials.

"Margaret Atwood speaking."

"I have always loved that name."

"Christ, Brian. What do you want?"

"I want to see you."

Margaret says nothing. She has no idea what to say. The snake speaks and Eve listens, as always.

"Margaret, I feel terrible. I need to see you so that we can talk things through. So we can make plans. We can't leave things the way they are."

Again, Margaret says nothing. She decides it is best to continue to wait this out.

"Margaret, I know this is not easy. Of course it isn't easy. What am I saying? What I'm trying to say is I would like to explain some things to you." No response.

"Look, I know I fucked up, I know that I am always fucking up, but I am what I am, right? I am sorry though for putting you through what I've put you through. And I would like to make amends somehow. The thing is I've been thinking about the divorce and I think I have a way to sort it out as quickly and painlessly as possible and for you to get what you deserve."

Margaret knows this is wrong. That it is false. But it is good to hear Brian act contrite, even if it is just acting. It is even good to hear his tired, old, hackneyed flirtation. That apple has always looked so delicious. Even when you can see the worms slithering in and out of it. Even when it is dripping with snake venom.

"Brian. I am at work now. I can't talk to you."

"Meet me for lunch tomorrow. I'll be at the Vietnamese place on Adelaide at noon. My treat."

Margaret pulls the phone slowly away from her ear and puts

it back in the cradle. She stares at it for several seconds afterward. She wants to resist the flood of unbidden Brian memories that are poised to run through her head now: Brian nude and laughing; Brian ugly and shouting; Brian flirting with other women; Margaret humiliating herself a thousand times over. The ridiculous pantomime played out with utter sincerity over and over again. Margaret was always the horse's ass. She was the one bumbling along in the dark behind Brian, while he played to the crowd. Prancing and whinnying and shaking his silky mane all the while.

She wishes she had the power to deliberately block memories, the power to cleanse her mind, at least in part. She would be content to have ten years of blank silence in place of her marriage. She would not miss it. Margaret likes blank.

Blank is her favourite colour.

Cranking up the Bob Sherman machine

BOB SHERMAN, HE'S OUR MAN! If he can't do it, no one can!

Bob Sherman sits at another desk, much like Brian's and less like Margaret's. He is wondering why he has agreed to do this thing. This is not exactly true: he knows why he has agreed. Rose and Ron are his friends and Margaret, well, Margaret has always been one of the most delightful creatures he has ever known and he has known her for her whole life. A thirty-five year period that has passed in a blink of his old, baggy eye. Margaret was one of those uncanny children that are wry and beautiful from the beginning; as a toddler, she could deliver a stony glare that was startling and hilarious to see. Her appeal in his view is obvious. It always was and still is boundless.

Yes, he knows why he has agreed to represent Margaret. He just isn't convinced that it is a very good idea. He knows Brian well and has known him, too, for a very long time. In fact, Bob Sherman has written a number of reference letters for Brian over the years, glowing ones. He has described him as he is: brilliant, crafty, effective and tireless. A worthy adversary. The thought of it makes Bob a little bit tired. Bob's own considerable skills are a little bit rusty, to be honest. He has been slowing down lately, taking on fewer and fewer cases, spending more time on the golf course. He wonders about his ability to crank up the great, hulking, puffing machine again, to get it to full speed, as surely will be required.

He groans. Puffs. Stretches and rolls his eyes. He pushes his chair away from his desk. He sputters and grumbles and a slow rumbling starts in his big, soft belly. A slow, chugging sound launches in his head and a smile twitches at the edges of his mouth.

Oh, what the hell, thinks Bob, let's roll. It's only Brian. Pipsqueak.

The dog bed

MARGARET AND BRIAN MEETING for lunch. It seems like a bad idea. She considers sending her mother instead – or her lawyer. Her fantasy is that she could go meet Brian and face off; that she could stay strong and calm and not break down and cry, not holler and pound her fists, not succumb. Out of sheer perversity she wonders if given the opportunity she could just pack up her things and go back to him. If she could just close down her sad, cold, boring apartment, hold her nose and go back home. If based on some cold promise from Brian that she could never believe, she could swallow that choking, giant, bitter pill that is her pride and go back there.

Could she sink that low? If her mother would let her? Possibly.

If she is honest with herself, she knows that it is possible. But it is worse than that: even if she were willing to debase herself in such an extraordinary way, Brian wouldn't even have her. She has been usurped. Someone has taken her place. Her dog bed at the foot of the master is occupied now. Good thing.

It is a strange thing to have a marriage end even if it wasn't a very good one. The future yawns before her now. She had thought that her life would play out in a certain way; she had thought that her future was set. She had not given her *future* a thought for many years. To marry is to dream, is to suspend disbelief. It is to allow the cynical self to be overridden and to have faith in the possibility of everlasting love, of love until death. Even if that love is awkward or disappointing, even if it causes pain, there is some comfort in knowing that you are part of a team. You know that if you get sick or helpless, someone will likely take care of you. You will not have to live your life alone, without input or opposition. But more than this, possibly more importantly, you know that you have a plan.

Margaret has always been a lover of plans, but now that the bottom has dropped out of things, she is sapped. She does not have the energy to think about her life. Everything is diminished. Her life has been reduced to a minute-by-minute carrying out of tasks. For what reason does she dress herself and work and feed herself and put money in the bank? To what end? She takes no joy from this life. At the moment, she finds it difficult to think of a single thing that she cares about. Except, she supposes, in a small, faintly glimmering way, her parents. She does not want to be a source of sadness or worry or disappointment to her parents. Is this enough to live a life for? Maybe not. How can she get something else? Should she bother?

Margaret turns to the files arranged on her desk and opens the closest one. Her eyes slide over the first page of text and register some inconsistencies in format. She reaches for her extra-fine-tipped red pen.

The big guns

THE ALIENS DO NOT LIKE THIS line of thinking. No good can come of it. They had thought that the whiteboard list had been a step forward, albeit a humble one. They had thought that the Leader's last visit had had a clear purpose, that it would have a lasting and positive impact. Now they see Margaret slipping and they worry. They worry, and so they caucus. Brainstorm. A more significant intervention is needed. There are some more radical methods they have used on humans in the past and have since abandoned: the abductions, the probes, the mind control. In the Leader's view, these have never been worth the trouble or the bad press.

The aliens have more tricks up their figurative sleeves, you can be assured. They have big guns. But these are not normally used to assist individual humans; they are usually reserved for broader effect. They have been called upon to prevent the odd oil spill or nuclear mishap, to meddle in a limited way in politics or armed conflicts. But, as everyone knows, the Leader is sweet on Margaret. It cannot be overstated: his focus is like a laser beam. The oceans could boil, mountains could crumble, gaping craters could open up and swallow every other human on the planet. For the moment, all earthly events will only be addressed by the Leader to the extent that they affect the life of Margaret Atwood.

The plan this time is unorthodox. It is unprecedented. There is some dissent. There is some whispered questioning of the Leader's motives, but mostly the aliens are beside themselves with excitement! How bold! What audacity! What *moxy*! Do they have enough time to carry it off? There are preparations to make, calculations to be done!

The ship is trembling with activity; the pulse of the aliens' frantic toil emanates in waves toward the earth. The tides rise just a little higher that night and hairline cracks spread across the crust of the earth.

Pocket-sized

BRIAN SITS AT HIS TABLE at the Noodle House, scrolling through e-mails on his BlackBerry. Marvellous devices, BlackBerrys. Their users give off an elegant hybrid of impressions: busy, impatient, aloof, all at once. A distinctly different flavour from that of a person texting on a cell phone. Though the difference in the actual activities is marginal, Brian supposes.

He is aware that Margaret will likely be late, that she will want to shame him in some small way. He doubts, however, that she will fail to show up altogether. It would be cowardly, an admission of defeat. He has made it easy for her to come – the restaurant is around the corner from her office and the service is fast. The booths are private, in case they want to make out. Just kidding! Brian laughs to himself at his own joke and types messages with his thumbs.

Margaret spots him from behind. It isn't like him to sit with his back to the door and it throws her off a little. She wishes that she could check her look in a mirror. Her dithering about her outfit today had been unprecedented. She had wanted to look good, but not flirtatious. She had wanted her outfit to say: here is a new Margaret, Brian, one that is much better now that you are out of her life. (She knew that, frankly, this was a lot to ask of an outfit.) And she had wanted the impossible – no matter what the magazines say – an outfit that makes her look more fit and trim than she actually is.

Back at her apartment, a pile of selected and discarded outfits covers her bed and spills onto her bedroom floor. In the end, she had chosen a crisp blue cotton dress and knee-high boots and now she regrets it. She wishes she had worn a suit, something more grown-up and serious. But it is too late. She tugs at her dress, straightens the belt, sucks in her stomach and strides toward the table.

Brian feels the rush of air as Margaret passes and slides into the bench across from him. He counts ten seconds before looking up from his Blackberry and smiling at her. She looks good, if a bit puffy around the eyes. Nice dress.

Margaret smiles with half her mouth and says hello. She lowers her eyes to the menu and starts flipping through. She had not anticipated it, but the sight of him has filled her with fury. She can feel a lump in her throat and tears are filling her eyes. Her mind casts around for some image, some trick that will bring her back on course, back to centre. Her vision blurs and a fat tear plops onto the plastic menu. She brushes it away with the cuff of her sleeve and clears her throat. Brian, mercifully, is not paying attention. Margaret tries to imagine that she is a great, huge, lumbering giant. She imagines that Brian is shrinking, that he becomes small enough to fit in the palm of her hand. That she could close her fist around him and squeeze.

Tiny Brian looks up from his menu and says she can order whatever she likes, it is his treat. And then, even before the waitress arrives to take their drink order, Brian begins his speech.

"OK, Margaret, I know you've hired Bob Sherman, which is great. Bob is a great guy, but if you want my opinion, we could both save a lot of money and heartache if we just work things out ourselves. I've drawn up some papers – don't freak out, they're not final." He is losing momentum, trying to read her expression. She has not said a word. She is sort of smiling, but not really. Is that a smirk?

"Read them over. Show them to Bob if you like, but you know I've had a lot of experience with these things and I promise you that if we invite other people into this process, it will get complicated and expensive. Margaret?" No response. She is smirking. His own smile is starting to hurt his face.

"Margaret, help me out here. Are you following?"

Margaret the Giant has faded out. She can't hear what he is saying any more. In her mind, she grabs her napkin, crushes it into a ball and forces it into Brian's mouth. She stands tall and flips the table over. Or, she hoists herself up onto the table, throws her head back and roars like a lion, howls like a wolf. She picks Brian up, squirming in her hand, and shoves him into her pocket.

Brian starts talking again. He reaches into his briefcase and extracts a large brown envelope, which he places on the table between them. Margaret leans across the table and puts both of her hands on top of Brian's. Startled into silence mid-sentence, Brian looks up and meets her gaze.

Through gritted teeth: "Brian, do not give me any *fucking papers.*"

"Margaret, be reasonable."

A little louder than necessary: "Brian, I am telling you: don't give me those fucking papers. I will scream. Put them back in your briefcase."

"Margaret."

"Stop saying my name and fucking put them back!"

"Just take them. Have a look at them later. If you don't like what's in them you can throw them out for Christ's sake! Calm down, *Jesus*! Don't you at least want to know if we can agree on things? Don't you want to at least try?"

Giant Margaret gets up, puts on her coat and walks out of the restaurant. Dishes rattle and the windows tremble. As she walks out the door, the ugly, bat-winged truth settles on her shoulders for the millionth (though the last) time: she is nothing to Brian.

He is an empty, horrible, greedy man that has never given a damn about her. He is blind and his heart is made of wood.

The outlaws

THE EARTH TURNS AND THE SUN rises on the day of the workshop. Margaret has been lying awake for hours wishing for death. The day that is beginning to form outside her window is steel grey. It is an appropriately cold, unkind November day. There is an uneasy feeling in her stomach. Her throat is parched and she can barely swallow. Perhaps she is ill, she thinks, knowing she is not. Oh, for a bout of good old-fashioned, undeniable vomiting flu! She rolls onto her side. Though it is unreasonably early, she can hear Rose rattling around in the kitchen, singing to herself. In the mirror on the closet door, Margaret spots the rumpled lump of her body under the covers. She sits up and faces herself. An immense plume of hair arches from the back of her head and there are dark circles under her eyes. She looks like a lunatic.

In the shower, Margaret is troubled once again by the question of wardrobe. What image does one wish to project at a seminar about *getting along* at work? She presumes that the event has been designed as a punishment of sorts; that the people in attendance have, like her, done something unseemly and have been sent there. Nobody would decide to take such a course of their own accord. A clutch of villains, then. Outlaws and assholes. People who don't know when enough is enough! Margaret feels that a number of costumes could work in these unusual circumstances: the gormless ingénue in a fluffy sweater that clearly could only offend someone by mistake; the polished executive in a suit that is just trying to get work done and people sometimes get in the way, for heaven's sake; the mousy wallflower who has clearly ended up in this workshop by mistake. Though all are tempting, in the end she opts to dress as she feels: like a sullen teenager. She pulls on her old, pink and black striped, hooded sweater and a tight, straight pair of jeans.

"Is that what you're wearing, sweetie?"

"It is."

"Why?"

"Because it seems like the right thing. Let it go, Mom."

"It's not what I would choose."

"Obviously."

"You don't think it would be better to wear something a bit more professional?"

"It's not a job interview, Mom, it's detention. Believe me, there won't be any *highflyers* there."

Margaret stares steadfastly into her cereal bowl. Rose lets it drop. At least Margaret is up and ready to go. At least it will be over. Soon.

Highflyers

THERE IS A BREAK IN THE CLOUDS and the aliens cheer as Margaret exits her building. The air is cold and crisp and the sun is brightening the sky. Margaret takes a shaky breath and heads toward the bus stop. The aliens had been worried that she might find a way to skip the seminar, but no! And they think she looks fantastic in her outfit – it is perfect. Everything is coming together perfectly.

The Leader, too, takes a shaky breath and lowers his head in a kind of prayer. He would like some kind of sign from the universe. He would like to know that he is doing the right thing, that his motives are pure. Around him, the ship is clattering with activity. There is a crazy pre-game atmosphere. He is humbled by the dedication of his crew. They have been working night and day to enact his crazy plan. They believe in him. And he has not been honest with them. Not entirely.

They think that their mission is to help Margaret, to help her until they are sure she will be alright without them. This is true.

They think that they are using extraordinary measures to accomplish this mission because Margaret is extraordinary, that she is needed on earth to carry out a secret and important task. This is also true.

They believe their intervention will be historic. That it will redeem the human race.

This, the Leader is less sure about.

The bleeder

Margaret slouches down low in her chair at a boardroom table with her course materials spread out before her. Fluorescent lights hum and buzz, casting a yellow-green light. The table is ever so slightly sticky to the touch.

Being the first of the condemned to arrive, she has fiddled with her notebook and pencil awkwardly for an excruciating fifteen minutes. She has watched her cohorts drift in, one by sorry one. She has kept tabs on the session facilitator out of the corner of her eye. The woman is gleamingly neat and tidy, a bright silk scarf knotted at her throat. She smiles with a mouthful of chiclet-like teeth and busybodies around the room, occasionally counting the participants to check if all are present. Margaret counts, too. If she includes herself, there are ten. Ten outlaws, nine of them men. Clearly most women know the rules, know how to keep it all in check. But not Margaret. She is a disappointment to the sisterhood of women once again.

Margaret looks at their wretched, mostly old faces. All with skin white as snow or paste. Relics. What embarrassing incidents have landed them here? She can well imagine. She anticipates a day filled with inappropriate comments and bewildered stares. But who is this arriving late, tumbling into the room?

This is a very unusual-looking man, and yet Margaret has an uncanny sense that she has seen him somewhere before.

In his favour, he is younger than the others. Quite likely he is around the same age as Margaret herself. His short, curly hair is red. Though the word red does not really do it justice. His hair is actually orange. It is in fact so orange that it appears to be transparent, to be lit from within. It is fibre-optic hair. His eyes are very dark and his eyebrows and eyelashes are truly white, his skin is so pale as to be bluish – where it is not freckled. How does she know him? Is it possible that he is from her home town? To Margaret's horror, he winks at her (*winks at her!*) and squeezes into the chair next to hers.

"Alright, then! That seems to be everyone. Let's get started." The voice is predictably piercing. "Could everyone please fill out the name tags provided and stick them on, so we can keep each other straight?"

Amid murmurs and grumbles, Magic Markers are taken up and names scrawled on adhesive labels, which are patted onto shirtfronts. Sheepish looks, nods of acknowledgement follow. Margaret takes note of the row of forgettable single-syllable men's names facing her: Rod, Jeff, Bob, Jim. With a sidelong glance, she confirms that her pale neighbour sports the unfamiliar and unlikely handle of Amos. She braces herself for what she knows will come next: the dreaded icebreaker activity that has launched every stupid corporate seminar in history.

Chiclet (who, according to her flower-festooned name tag, is really named Tammy) leans over and places both palms on the table. Then, she delivers the speech she has delivered a thousand times, carefully modulating her voice so as to sound human.

"Good morning, everybody! Welcome to Working Together: Difference in the Workplace! I look forward to getting to know all of you and I hope you will be able to relax and enjoy yourselves a little. Hey – at least you're not at the office, right?"

Blank stares from all directions.

Tammy straightens up, tugs on the bottom of her jacket that is riding up, and continues.

"The overriding focus, the philosophy of this session will be *positivity*. There will be no beating ourselves up and no criticizing of others: this is a *criticism-free zone*. I think you will find that the key to harmony – inside ourselves, in our homes and in our workplaces – is to consciously and consistently focus on the positive in everyone. Now, enough of my preaching! Who would like to kick things off by telling the group your name, your job and just for fun, something you like about yourself?"

The response to this invitation is dead silence. Margaret sneaks a quick look around the table and confirms that all participants are staring at the table before them, stubbornly resisting eye contact with any other human in the room. A chair leg grinds against the floor as one of the Jeffs shifts his significant, uncomfortable weight. Margaret is swallowing hard to suppress a sudden urge to clear her throat, which she fears could be interpreted as a way of volunteering to 'kick things off.' She stares at the table and starts counting slowly and silently. She reaches an amazing twenty-seven before Tammy barks with laughter. All heads bobble and swivel toward her.

"Such a quiet group! Well, let's start with me then. As you already know, my name is Tammy Howard and I am an aspiring author, a community volunteer and a motivational speaker! What do I like about myself?" She taps her long nails on the table, looks at the ceiling, nods. "One of the things I like about myself is that I have always been able to *connect* with people, even if we don't always have much in common."

Connect. Margaret wants to vomit. She is pretty sure that she and Tammy have very little in common – apart from their species, race and gender – and doubts they will be able to connect with each other in any way, whatever the hell that means. And thank God for that.

"OK! Let's go to my right and work our way around the table." Margaret realizes with some relief that this will mean she will be second-last.

Her fellow workshoppers struggle through their short speeches. Throughout, she feels short of breath and her hands are trembling. She laces her fingers together and squeezes hard. She looks down at her lap and thinks, thinks, thinks about what she could possibly say that she likes about herself. She digs at a hangnail on her right thumb and is only half-conscious of the deep drone of the men's voices grudgingly putting forward their humble attributes for consideration by the group. Jim offers that he is a good father and grandfather. Rod mostly does what he's told and tries to do a good job. Margaret would like to say that she is quiet, that she doesn't cause people too much trouble, but lately this hasn't been exactly true. She thinks of her mother, miles away from home, crying in her lap and she thinks of their old family friend Bob Sherman spending his time labouring on her divorce instead of spending it strolling around the golf course. She thinks, reluctantly, of how deeply and needlessly she hurt the feelings of her co-worker Marie.

Very likely, she is causing Brian some trouble, but she feels fine about that.

She picks at her thumb and winces as she pulls off a long strip of cuticle. The group is loosening up now, is laughing and joshing as the wave of conversation flows toward her.

The room quiets as Tammy and the men await Margaret's contribution. She tries to think of something meaningless to say that will cause the focus of the room to skip lightly over her. Her thumb is bleeding. She closes her left fist tightly around it.

"My name is Margaret, I..." and here she is interrupted by the trumpeting voice of Tammy.

"Margaret has a very *distinguished* name, everybody. I thought I might have someone very famous in my group when I saw the list!" A trill of laughter and an expectant look at Margaret follows. All eyes turn toward her. Margaret stares daggers at Chiclet. In her mind she is getting up and walking out of the room, down the corridor, out the door and down the street to the bus stop. Screw this.

"Go ahead, Margaret. Tell everybody!"

"Atwood. My last name is Atwood. It's not an unusual name, you know. There are thousands and thousands of us. And there are plenty of Margarets, too." She is not sure where she is going with this. She can feel heat rising from her waist all the way up to her hairline. Her scalp feels prickly. Her ginger neighbour is nodding hard at her. So hard she believes he might be having a seizure. "My parents had never even heard of Margaret Atwood when I was born. It was a mistake. It's a pain in the ass if you want to know." There is some scowling at this, some raised eyebrows. It is clear that her audience had thought they might have some fun with this Margaret Atwood thing, but seeing that none is forthcoming, they are losing interest. "Right. Where was I? My name is Margaret, I am a proofreader in the communications department of an insurance company and I don't know what I like about myself. I guess I like that I work hard even though I don't care about my job. Even though it doesn't really matter to me, I still do a good job."

Tammy pauses and gives Margaret a bemused look – this doesn't really sound genuinely positive to her – but decides to move along.

As the group's focus shifts to her neighbour, Margaret looks down and sees that blood from her torn hangnail is leaking between the fingers of her closed fist. Amos slips her a tissue underneath the table and clears his throat.

"My name is Amos, I am a salesman and I happen to be excellent at eating pie," he says, grinning idiotically. "I could do it all day long!"

The room evaporates into laughter and chatter and within minutes the exercise is miraculously over. The group is released for a five-minute break. Margaret pushes her chair away from the table and bolts for the ladies' room.

Positivity!

Margaret will not leave the ladies' room until she is certain that the break is over. She carefully peels the tissue off her thumb and surveys the damage. Her hands are covered with bright red sticky blood. The gelatinous beginning of a scab is forming at the base of her thumbnail. Gingerly, she washes and dabs at the wound with a paper towel. She tears off a narrow strip of paper, folds it and wraps it tightly around her thumb. If only she were the sensible kind of lady that carries Band-Aids in her purse. Margaret stares at her face in the mirror. She is not that kind of lady at all.

She is killing time. She does not wish to get involved in any break-time corridor chit-chat. As an extra precaution, she digs her earphones out of her purse, inserts them and turns the volume up loud for her short walk from the bathroom to the boardroom. The music creates a tinny halo of noise around her head, a force field against any unwanted advances. Sex Pistols, "Anarchy in the UK." There could be no other choice.

Nothing else is ugly enough. *Rrrrrrrrright!*

Back in the boardroom, the men are relaxed, laughing. Apparently, they are resigned to their fate and have decided they might as well enjoy themselves. Margaret takes her prickly place among them, a human cactus. Tammy strides back into the room, ready to deliver the gospel of positivity. She claps her hands, stands up straight and tall and lays it on, thick and sugary as frosting on a grocery store birthday cake.

"*Alrighty then!* Now that we've all given some thought to some of our own wonderful qualities, let's see if we can find out what we like about each other!"

Margaret rolls her eyes. She will probably get a cramp from rolling her eyes, from so much sneering. Is that possible? Once again, she wonders what would happen if she left, just cut her losses and headed for the door. Tammy would certainly take note and report back to Lenny or some drone in the human resources department. Would she get fired? Probably not. Would she get any credit for attending part of the workshop? Would they send her, oh my God, to another one to make up for it?

"For the next exercise, I have divided you into pairs. Rod, because we have an uneven number, you can be my partner for this one. The rest of you will find a little yellow sticky note in front of you marked with a letter. Please find the person who has the same letter, introduce yourselves and we'll get to work!"

Margaret's sticky note says *D*. It feels like her grade – just barely passing. She looks around the room to see Grandpa Jim smiling and heading toward her with a *D* stuck to his raised index finger. Perfect. They are bound to *connect*. Around the room, people are standing in awkward pairs, awaiting instruction. They learn that they will be sharing their workplace metaphors with each other. Sandwich time at long last. As Jim and Margaret head for a corner of the room to settle in for a painfully forced conversation about the symbolic roles they play in their respective workplaces, as expressed through painfully forced metaphors, she looks over her shoulder to see who is paired with Amos. He is across the room, laughing like a hyena with the enormous Jeff. They are slapping each other's shoulders and doubling over. How can it be so easy for some people? How do they shake off the embarrassment of being themselves, ignore the distastefulness of all that is human and just *get along*?

There is nothing in Margaret that is able to go with the flow.

She is all opposition.

One hundred percent resistance.

Better out than in

AFTER LUNCH — WHICH MARGARET has spent eating a slice of pizza behind a giant tropical plant in the corner of the atrium of an office building six blocks away — they are gathered around the table again.

The exercise they are about to undertake, Tammy tells them, is the most important one of the day. It will allow them to 'reintegrate' into the workplace, having fully worked through their 'issues.' They will be equipped with new strategies for working with others. Margaret can hardly wait. But it gets worse. One by one, they will be expected to share with the entire group the odious behaviour that has landed them in this workshop. Then, with the help of the group, they will (a) identify why what they did was inappropriate and (b) brainstorm what a more appropriate approach to the situation might be.

Margaret was not prepared for this. Was it really necessary to rehash that tired, old crucifixion chestnut again? She was pretty sure that she had learned all she could from that particular experience.

And you know what else? She didn't want to hear about the misdeeds of others either.

But look out. Here it comes.

Rod had told a co-worker to "stop being such a Jew" because he had been proposing cost-saving measures. Jim had suggested that "getting laid" might relieve the stress of some of his female co-workers. Bob had *mooned his boss* at the annual staff picnic.

The revelations are put forward and the group dutifully follows instructions by making careful attempts to explain why these were not good, professional practices and offering suggestions for alternative approaches. Like keeping your big trap shut, thinks Margaret, like never speaking to anyone ever again. From the sidelines, Tammy the Cheerleader makes cheerful interjections about how everyone makes mistakes! And nobody's perfect!

As Margaret listens to the confessions of her fellow sinners, an upsetting notion is forming in her mind. These people are bad, but she is worse. They are stupid and hateful, but they had offended others *by mistake*. (OK, maybe not the mooner. He probably knew exactly what we was doing.) But, she had been hateful by design. She had contrived her offensive joke, practiced it, honed it and delivered it to her audience, expecting to get some laughs.

Maybe she won't tell her story, after all. Maybe she can come up with a new one on the spot, something more palatable. But she is short on ideas. All the best ones have been taken already.

As the table turns to her, she begins. Her voice is flat and loud.

"I was standing at the photocopier with a bunch of my co-workers, when someone commented on my psoriasis." She holds her hands up crusty palms out to demonstrate. Winces around the table. She nods in agreement. "Pretty gross, I know. I joked that it was stigmata." Half of her fellow participants nod, half look confused.

"You know, an Easter miracle, happens to nuns sometimes. Like the crucifixion." Murmurs. Nods. Some head-shaking.

"Well, anyway. Turns out one of my new co-workers is pretty religious. Christian. And she was really upset. I didn't even notice …" Margaret is both laughing and crying as she trails off, shaking her big donkey head. Hee-haw! My name is Ass. And this is my story.

She endures the group's input on what exactly it was she had done wrong – as if she didn't know – and their suggestions for a better approach (the aforementioned technique of keeping one's trap shut). With mercy, the world moves on. Her relief is great. She is glad she told the real story after all. Better out than in, she thinks. Maybe there is something to this confession thing. And with any luck, she will never see any of these people again.

To her right, Amos is admitting to posting homemade signs around the office as a way of venting his frustration with his co-workers' bad behaviour. It had started politely: **Please keep your voice down – others are TRYING to work!** But as months wore on, the signs became increasingly rude: **PLEASE SHUT UP! NOBODY CARES ABOUT YOUR STUPID LIFE!** Margaret is at a loss to explain why this approach is inappropriate. She likes it just fine.

A full hour later, Tammy is delivering her end-of-session

prattle. Margaret is trying to zone out, to replace her words with song lyrics or pure, fuzzy static. She tries to block all incoming information, but she will fail. She will suffer the trite lessons one more time, lessons that every fifth-grader knows and no thinking adult could, in Margaret's view, possibly implement. *See the best in others. Believe in yourself. Think before you speak.*

The boardroom clock finally, grudgingly reaches the hour, the magical moment when they are set free, turned loose to sin again. Margaret gathers up her things and leaves without a word. Never has any exit from any room been so thrilling. She feels that her feet are hovering an inch or so above the ground as she peels away.

The cactus and the fruitcake

IMPOSSIBLY, HE IS THERE at the bus stop before her. Amos. Waiting. He raises an eyebrow at her and smiles a big smile. "Going my way?"

"Looks like it," says Margaret wanting to disintegrate him with her eyes. Wanting to set fire to him with her brain. She puts her earphones in and turns the music up, up, up. Save me, rock and roll, this one last time. Remove this creature from my personal sphere.

As summoned, Patti Smith fills her ears, wailing "Break It Up!" Margaret thinks she can hear the thump of her fist pounding on her chest as she sings. It gives her chills. She lets a few moments pass and tentatively raises her eyes to see if her hint has been taken, if her new, persistent companion has vanished. She is astonished to see that he is still there, that he is looking at her. He is, in fact, still talking to her. She pulls the earphones out, music spilling into the air, and stares frankly at him.

"She's right, you know. She's an idiot, obviously, but I think she's right."

"*Who*?"

"Tammy. The facilitator."

In spite of herself, Margaret can't resist asking: "How could she possibly be right about anything?"

"About being positive. About seeing the good in others. It isn't natural, of course, or clever, but it might make a person less miserable."

"Whatever." Margaret rolls her eyes.

"Look, it's easy to see everything that's wrong with the world. Any idiot knows that people are shitty. But it is equally obvious that people are good. If you look for it, you can find that, too. So, what if you could brainwash yourself to ignore bad things and focus on good things? It might make you feel better. At least part of the time, anyway. I might try it."

Margaret nods and turns away. Her bus, thank God, is coming. She is ready at the door as it comes to a halt in front of her. The doors open and she bounds up the steps, heads as far into the recesses of the bus as possible and lands heavily in a seat at the back. It is crammed with teens and other troublemakers. She looks up to see Amos heading toward her, index finger in the air, as though he were mid-sentence.

He squeezes into the seat with her and there they sit, thigh against thigh, shoulder against shoulder. The cactus and the fruitcake.

"OK," he says, "OK. Next person that gets on, find something you like about them. Ready?"

Margaret cranks her head around and stares at him. Amos is undeterred.

"Here's one. I like ... I like the way she lets the hairs grow on her chin. It shows strength of character. Oh. Another one. I like his jacket – it makes him look like a fighter pilot or something. Alright, you try."

Margaret sighs and looks down the aisle at the next passenger boarding the bus. It is a teenage girl with giant hoop earrings and unbelievably low-riding jeans. "I like the way her mother let her out of the house like that."

"Try again."

"No thanks."

"Just one more. Try."

Margaret realizes that it will be easier – less trying – to comply. She scopes out the next victim. A man in his fifties, in a dapper, black overcoat, carrying something (his lunch?) neatly tied in a red handkerchief. "I like his handkerchief parcel. It's mysterious. It gives him a vagabond quality."

Margaret can't help but wonder, in this day and age, in these days of insulated lunch bags and briefcases and backpacks, why a person carries something in a knotted handkerchief. Is he a lonely man that has – left to his own devices – come up with this cockamamie way of packing his lunch? Is it something his crazy wife does for him in an attempt to be cute?

"Well done," says Amos. "Now it's my turn."

And so they will continue, with varying degrees of sincerity and enthusiasm, until suddenly the bus is approaching Margaret's stop. She rings the bell and scrambles over him. He raises a hand to wave, but she is already rushing down the aisle to the door. He watches her go and silently lists all the things he likes about her. He likes her hair, her walk, her sneakers. Her smell, her laugh, her mouth. Her cranky bad attitude. He likes the whole hot mess.

Margaret steps onto the sidewalk and into the damp, quiet November gloaming. Instead of looking back at him, she looks up at her building, yellow lights already burning in most of the windows.

She can feel his eyes on the back of her head.

The side of her that had been pressed against him, that had felt so uncomfortably hot on the bus, is clammy and cold in the night air.

The imposter

AMOS HAS A SECRET. He has two secrets, actually, but one is such a secret he doesn't even know about it yet.

Maybe he never will.

The Leader will do his very best to make sure he doesn't. The secret Amos knows about is this: he has never done anything at the office that would be offensive enough to land him in a 'tolerance seminar.' He has never even worked in an office. He runs his own business, a store downtown. He is polite to everyone he talks to every day – his customers, his staff, the courier guy. Everyone. He has never made an off-colour joke, never pinched or fondled anyone, never abused his very limited power in any way. So why, you might ask, was Amos at that seminar with Margaret?

Simple. He is a plant, an imposter. And Tammy 'the Chiclet' Howard is his sister-in-law. Because one of the many things Amos is not very good at is saying no. Especially to Tammy.

Ah, Tammy. Where to begin? His brother's wife is a piece of work. He wishes she were one in a million, but even Amos knows better than this. Turn on the TV any day of the week and you will see many, many more of her ilk. Smiling through their tears with their perfect, white teeth. Beautiful women who feel ugly, who try too hard at everything. Tammy is loud, nervous and generally hard to be around, but somehow you want to help her. You want to tell her to relax, that it will all be OK. You want to tell her to eat a sandwich so that her bird-like bones don't break right through her skin.

"Amos, what are you doing Monday?"

"I'm taking the day off."

"I know, but what are you doing? Do you have any plans?"

Tammy knows that Amos rarely has any plans. Amos's brother, Michael, is smirking across the dinner table at him. He is the king of his castle and Tammy is his shrill, frantic queen. No one here gets out alive.

"Not really, no." He knows there is no point in lying, that he has no believable story ready. The roast beef is delicious but he can tell it will not be worth what he is about to get himself wrangled into. No such thing as a free lunch, as the saying goes.

"I'm doing another workshop and was wondering if you could come along. Lighten things up a bit."

Amos has been to eleven of Tammy's positivity-personality-rainbow seminars and has secretly enjoyed every minute of them. He likes creating a slightly different persona for each session. Each session he likes to push it a bit further, to see how weird his contributions to the discussion can get before Tammy calls him on it, before the jig is up. He also enjoys hearing about people's lives, the mistakes they have made, their confusion about the rules of polite society. He has been surprised to find how compelling he finds almost every story, how easy it is to sympathize. It complicates morality when you realize mostly people don't mean to be bastards. It makes outrage more difficult. Mostly.

He has also found, to his surprise, that Tammy's goofy positivity message has infiltrated his daily thinking and, he can hardly believe this, has seemed to actually make him happier. Maybe it is just the repetition, a kind of brainwashing. It doesn't really seem possible that being happy is as simple as deciding to focus on what is good in the world and not on what is bad. It is too easy. But maybe for Amos right now being happy is as simple as focussing his longing on one positive thing. On one woman who is just bad enough to be sent to one of Tammy's workshops.

"You know you like it. Big loser. Why don't you just say yes?"

"What?" Amos stares at his brother, pretending to be shocked.

"You love it. Just go already."

"Why would I love being a fake participant in a stupid tolerance workshop? Sorry Tammy." Tammy shrugs.

"Because you're pathetic, maybe?" Michael grins with mashed potato across his front teeth. "Because you can't get enough of Tammy's mad workshop skills?"

"Actually, I just remembered I have to do something."

"Liar."

Is it really lying? He does have something to do. He wants to stay home and dream. He wants to stay home all day and pine for love. For the love of Margaret Atwood. Is that so wrong?

"No really. It's important. I'll go to the next one, Tammy. I promise." He gets up and starts clearing dishes as the king of the castle pushes his chair back from the table and regards his brother with frank suspicion.

(The second secret, the one that Amos doesn't know about, is that he is a target.

The Leader has been watching him.

He is watching him right now.

He is ready to do something he has never done before.

He is going to dive right into Amos and take possession.

He is going to give this budding earthling love a little nudge in the right direction.

And he is really, really going to enjoy himself.)

The chandelier over the table flickers off and on again. As Amos carries his stack of dishes toward the kitchen a strange feeling comes over him. He feels doubled, as though there are hands inside his hands, feet inside his feet. There is a slight delay in all of his movements, as though the film of his life is a frame or two behind the soundtrack. His foot catches the edge of the rug and he is stumbling, struggling to get his balance. He clutches the dirty plates to his chest and tries to contain the momentum that is sending him running, thundering toward his sister-in-law who is standing at the kitchen sink. Hoping to miss her, he tucks and rolls, somersaulting across the kitchen floor.

When the lights go out, Amos is lying on his back, still pressing the dirty dishes to his chest, his shirt soaked through with gravy. None of his bones are broken. All of the plates are, miraculously, intact. Tammy is still standing, stunned, by the kitchen sink, looking down at him. Michael's belly laugh rises out of the darkness of the dining room and is caught by Tammy, and then by Amos. Tammy's fluffy, little dog clicks excitedly across the tile floor to Amos, sniffs his right ear, his neck, down his chest and starts licking his gravy-coated fingers.

Blackout

THE FLUORESCENT LIGHTS twitch and dim as Margaret climbs the stairs. By the time she reaches her apartment all the lights in the building are out. The hallway is suddenly quiet and she listens. If she strains she can hear the faintest ticking in the air, the building responding to the darkness, the slow cooling down of everything.

She presses her ear against the door and hears only her own breath. Feeling around in her purse, Margaret locates her keys. She runs her fingers over the key to find the flat side and guides it into the lock. Once inside, she stands with her back against the door. Her eyes adjust slowly to the gloom. The weak last light of the day comes in through the windows. "Mom?"

"In the kitchen!" Rose stands like a statue in the middle of the kitchen floor and Margaret stands by the door, both women waiting for the lights to come back on, afraid to move in case they blunder into something. They wait a minute more. Nothing. Margaret carefully makes her way across the living room to the window and looks out. She sees no lights: no lights on the block, possibly no lights in the entire city. The buildings are black columns. Above them is the great expanse of the greying autumn evening sky. To call it a sunset would be a lie. The sun is slowly erasing itself, vanishing into a grey-black starless night.

Rose picks her way across the living room and joins Margaret at the window and the two breathe quietly, ears cocked for some noise to break the unfamiliar silence. Rose slides her arm around Margaret's waist and puts her head on her shoulder. Very, very lightly, covertly, she touches her nose to the fabric of Margaret's sweater and breathes contentedly inward. Her love for her daughter is a kind of non-stop radiant heat. There is no turning it off. Margaret smiles in the dark and thinks that she likes her mother when she is like this, when she is nice and when she is quiet.

For once, in the city, the only sounds they can hear come from living things: a distant human voice, a dog barking, a baby crying. Then, before long, there is a chunk and then a whir and the whole apartment, the whole block is turned on. The light is painfully bright. The vibrating hum of the appliances, the fans, the motors, the filaments inside the bulbs, all add up to an astounding din. Margaret and Rose look at each other and laugh out loud. The food in the fridge is a bit warmer, the meat in the freezer is just a little bit soft around the edges. There is half-cooked macaroni and cheese in the oven, but it will be fine. It will all work out in the end. The aliens are certain of this.

Rose heads to the kitchen and pours two generous glasses of wine. Margaret walks across the floor to the whiteboard and with her old sweater sleeve pulled over her hand wipes off the first two items on the list. Workshop prepared for, attended and survived.

She takes a moment to reflect and then erases the third one, too – Bob Sherman engaged, bastard about to be launched from her life for good.

Six

Don't show your belly

"Does that all make sense, then?"

Margaret examines the leathery old saddlebag face of Bob Sherman. It is a fascinating topography – knolls and craters and winding roads. Wrinkles, lumps and bags. She rests her hand against her own cheek, which feels soft and smooth. Bob's face looks like it is made of something different, something rubbery and tough. His head is as big as a bear's; his hands are thick, meaty paws.

She remembers, as a child, marvelling at the size of those hands. They could make a sandwich look like it was the size of a saltine, a beer mug like a thimble.

"Pretty much," says Margaret. "Now what?"

"Now you sign all the copies, we serve Brian with the papers and see how big a fight we have on our hands. Ready?" He pulls his jowly mug into a big smile.

Margaret thinks so and signs her name over and over again. Never could she have imagined such a thing: a human relationship, so full of hope and romance and magic and pain and suffering, condensed into this carefully-worded contract, this statement of rights and accounts. She finds it both dismally sad and immensely satisfying. Thank God for Bob Sherman. How much more horrible it would be to wade through this stinking bog alone. She would never find the strength. She would lay down in the filth and let the water fill her lungs.

She would roll over and show Brian her pale belly and hope that he would not go for her throat.

Or show it

THEN AGAIN, MARGARET THINKS, sometimes there is really nothing to be done except roll over and show your belly.

If that's what it takes, that is what she will do. She is sitting in Lenny's office, in the chair he has waved his hand at, and she is waiting for him to get off the phone. She is silently rehearsing her speech.

Lenny, for his part, is struggling to pay attention to what his wife is saying to him (as he knows that he will be tested on this information later) while trying to think of a way to gently wrap the conversation up so he can get on with his day. *Yes, he will pick up milk. No, he will not forget. Yes, he will be home on time. Yes, he will drive Becky to her friend's house.* Yes, he will do a million niggling little things to make her life a bit easier. Yes. Yes. Yes, honey. Yes.

Margaret pulls the left sleeve of her sweater up to her elbow and rolls her arm outward on her lap. She has transcribed the whiteboard list onto the inside of her forearm with a ballpoint pen in minuscule block capital letters. Consistent with the list at home, she has drawn a straight line through items one through three. She will focus today's efforts on item four: setting things straight at the office. Though she has entertained the idea of having the list actually tattooed onto her arm – a new permanent line engraved on her flesh to mark each milestone – she has decided against it. It is probably best that it fades as she goes along. She pulls her sleeve back down.

Lenny murmurs into the phone, a bearded prune propped in a fancy leather swivel chair. He puts the phone down and turns to Margaret expecting the worst: a complaint or a resignation. People so rarely come to his office to tell him something good – least of all Margaret. He is already wondering how he will replace her if she leaves or, alternatively, what accusation he may have to defend himself against.

"Lenny, I'm getting divorced."

He is not sure what this is; it could be an introduction to a resignation. Or a request for time off. He waits for her to continue.

"And I haven't really been handling it very well. I haven't been myself." Margaret begins to feel embarrassed, her face is reddening, but she pushes through. "I just wanted to let you know that I am really sorry for what I said, for upsetting Marie. And that I like my job and I will keep working hard and I will try to get along with people." Damn. She is crying now.

Lenny pushes a box of tissues at her and looks down at his hands resting on the desk. He hates it when women cry – he always feels like it is his fault somehow. It makes him want to squeeze them tight which of course he is never allowed to do. He looks at Margaret and thinks about what it would be like to squeeze her. It seems as though she has diminished in the last month, she looks shrunken. She used to have a more buxom, milkmaid kind of look. Now, to his mind, she looks a bit more sinewy and tough. Perhaps a bit meaner, in spite of the tears. He decides not to give too much away too quickly.

"I presume you have spoken to Marie?"

"Not yet. But I will. Today. I want to get it over with."

"Good thinking. Well, let me know how it goes." He turns to the work on his desk as if she is already gone.

Margaret stands up. "Thanks, Lenny."

Lenny nods like a tough guy and Margaret leaves his office. She thinks about how she would like to hate him, but doesn't. He is too sad to hate, too captive. Like he is dragging around a trap on his leg.

An army of girls

MARIE IS CRYING. NOT JUST A LITTLE BIT, either. Tears are falling onto her desk like raindrops – plop, plop, plop. Margaret stops dead in front of her desk. "Marie?"

"Oh, *screw you*, Margaret."

Margaret is truly shocked by this. "What? Marie, what's the matter?"

"Like you care."

This is not going the way Margaret had pictured it: her humble apology, followed by Marie's grudging acceptance and maybe some superficial chatty camaraderie. Evidently, there is another factor at play in Marie's life today, one that is surely none of Margaret's business. She wonders if she can return to her desk and try again later. She makes a half-turn toward the corridor.

"Margaret, wait."

"Marie, I don't want to bother you. I can see you have other things going on. I just wanted to ..." Marie is not listening to her. Not really. Her beautiful, shiny eyes are pointed in Margaret's direction, but the blinds are pulled down. Out to lunch. Back in five. Margaret thinks she might as well keep going now that she's started. "I just wanted to apologize for upsetting you when I made that joke. It was stupid. I have been thinking about it a lot and I know I was completely out of line. I really didn't ..." Marie's face is blank. Without fully meaning to, Margaret shifts tactics. "OK, Marie. Listen. How about I take you to lunch? You hungry?"

Without a word, without any discernible facial expression, Marie hauls herself out of her chair as though she weighs a thousand pounds. She heaves a sigh – golden-haired head hung low, chin on chest – and slouches over to the coat tree. She slumps into her red wool jacket, then she stares at Margaret and waits to be led away like a child. Because she doesn't care anymore. Because nothing is right anymore. Because she has done something catastrophic. Everything for Marie is different now, tangled in knots.

As Margaret will find out, Marie was contacted by a police officer last week. This special detective informed Marie that Tom Francis had been charged with a number of crimes. Tom Francis, her sole companion as a teenager, her friend and abuser. Apparently, he had abducted and sexually assaulted an eleven-year-old girl. Tom had known the girl from church – she was a member of the Teens and Tweens for Christ group that he had established in the small northern town he had been living in these past few years. The two had gone missing simultaneously. The girl had failed to come home after school and Tom had failed to show up at work the next day. Police had found his truck parked outside a motor lodge on the highway ten miles outside of town. The girl had been missing for a total of eighteen hours and she had a story to tell. And she was not the only one.

Investigators began to follow the trail of Tom Francis back through the years, through a number of small communities and small churches. The list of names grew, ending with sweet Marie. One by one, an army of girls and women told stories to weary police officers, and when Marie was contacted, she went ahead and told her story, too. She went to an office downtown that felt more like a cell and told several strangers everything she could remember about Tom Francis. Everything she had never told anyone. And her parents were furious with her. They had asked her if she had thought about what she was doing, if she had thought about the impact it might have on them and on their church. They told her that she had better be sure about what she was saying because a man's reputation was at stake. They recommended that she look deep into her soul and take responsibility for her own actions and that she pray to the Lord for forgiveness. Marie had endured this in silence.

Marie realizes that the road ahead is terrible and lonely and that it could take a very long time to arrive at some peace. She may have to tell her story many times, and she will have to relive it each time. She may have to see his face and speak the truth to it and she will not speak with strength and conviction. She will be confused, knowing that in a strange, sickening way she had loved him. Even now she hates-but-loves him. She prays for his soul.

Marie knows only one thing with certainty. She knows that she will have to leave home. She cannot come undone in her parents' house. They are not on her side right now.

Hours have passed and Margaret and Marie are sitting across from each other in this cafeteria-style restaurant. Tables are strewn with trays and crumpled napkins. A stampede of wild horses has thundered through and now the dust has settled. The air is clear and quiet. Marie's hot, moist hands are in Margaret's hands. They are both holding on tight. They will not go back to work today. Neither one of them is feeling very well.

Flight

Margaret tells the cab to wait as she and Marie head into the house. It is, as Margaret expected, spotlessly clean and full of the Lord. Crucifixes, needlepoint bible verses, palm fronds, and it smells powerfully of disinfectant. Margaret can taste baby powder on her tongue.

Marie's room is small and bright and tidy. There is a desk in the corner with a wicker chair. There is a plastic lamp that has a frolicking cartoon lamb on the shade. There are ruffled curtains and a ruffled bedspread and ruffled pillows, all baby blue and white lace. It is no place for a twenty-two-year-old woman, thinks Margaret. No place for anyone sane. She spots a purple stuffed dinosaur tucked into the corner of the book shelf and she feels old. She feels like a mother.

For a moment Marie stands in the middle of the room and Margaret is struck, not for the first time, by her formidable beauty. Marie is not beautiful like a fashion model or a Barbie doll; she is beautiful like a mountain range or a peacock or a rose. She is undeniable natural beauty, young and strong and perfect. She attracts all eyes, everywhere she goes. It makes people feel good to look at her.

Marie heads for the closet and pulls out a hard-sided, olive-green suitcase and opens it on the bed. She begins to fill it with neatly folded clothes. She will only take clothing – no books, no jewellery, no mementos. She wants to leave something of herself behind and start fresh.

Margaret is clearing out dresser drawers, gathering up little stacks of white cotton underpants and placing them on the bed beside the suitcase for Marie. Piles of paired socks, pyjama sets, fuzzy sweaters – mostly purchased, she assumes, by Marie's soon to be traumatized parents. The thought of them makes the hair on the back of Margaret's neck stand up. What is she doing in their house, helping their daughter run away? Why is nothing ever clearly right or wrong? Why does it seem like every action taken to benefit one person comes at a cost to others? It is as though there is only so much happiness in the world and if you want more, you have to take it from someone else.

"Margaret?"

"Yeah?"

"Come here for a minute." Marie snaps the suitcase closed and turns toward her. She takes Margaret's clammy psoriasis-scarred hands in hers. "Let's pray together before we go."

"OK," says Margaret, "but I won't mean it."

"Sure you will." Marie closes her eyes and bows her head, squeezing Margaret's hands tight. Margaret closes her eyes, too. What would her co-workers say if they could see her now? She fidgets. What would her mother think? Or Brian? What on earth is she doing?

Marie clears her throat. "Dear Lord, please give me strength to find my way in this world. Give me direction. Make me equal to the challenges that lay ahead. Please help my parents to understand my actions and help us to be a family again. And, Lord, help my friend Margaret, as she is helping me. She is lost, Lord. Help her open her heart and mind so she can find her path forward. Amen."

If praying is wishing then Margaret supposes that she does mean it after all. She wishes for all those things. But she knows it will hurt to open her heart and mind. It hurts already. Her mother, Marie, that Amos guy, all trying to get in there. All jamming a thumbnail hard into that first hairline crack.

The cabbie is leaning on the horn now, causing the birds to flutter out of the treetops and into the sky. Margaret grabs the suitcase and looks at her accomplice. The two women hustle out the front door, down the sidewalk and into the cab like burglars. As the car pulls onto the wide, deserted suburban street, the bandits look at each other and grin. It is strangely thrilling to be on the loose, midday on a weekday, playing hooky. Sun is pouring in through the windows making them and everything around them shine. Margaret opens the window just a crack and closes her eyes.

The sun and the breeze, the hum of the car and the weight of her purse on her lap all seem perfect. It is a perfect day for flight.

The magic number

Rose shakes her head and goes to the white board. With slow careful movements she erases Item Number Six: Be less boring. Surely this is the least boring thing her daughter has ever done. Very surprising indeed. Margaret and Marie are laughing and chatting in the kitchen, chopping vegetables and browning meat. According to Marie, her stew is famous in certain circles. Rose heads to the guest room to change the sheets. She will sleep on the couch for now. She imagines she will be going home soon anyway. There is not much left on the board now – only really a haircut, she supposes. Margaret can handle that one on her own. Though you wouldn't know to look at her these days. Her hair is long and wild.

The aliens gaze on this scene with smiles on their green faces and tears in their eyes. They stand with their scaly hands clasped together over their hearts. What a remarkable development! They could not have predicted this! They could not be more pleased. And they are very grateful because it has been a difficult few days for them. The Leader has been acting strangely and their faith has been shaken. They fear that he is deviating from the plan. That he has gone rogue again. He has been blocking his thoughts from them, disappearing for hours at a time. Not encouraging. But now this! Maybe, just maybe, the addition of Marie to the household was somehow the Leader's doing and everything is on track after all. They decide to believe it. They will relax for the evening and watch the ladies of apartment 306.

Unlikely earth flower

IN ANOTHER APARTMENT just a few blocks down the street, the Leader is making his own dinner. Curried lamb is simmering on the back burner, fragrant basmati rice on the front. A bottle of red wine is uncorked and breathing on the counter. He sings himself a little song as he tosses the salad. He throws in a handful of sunflower seeds and reaches into the bag for more. Imagine sunflower seeds! Imagine the unlikely towering flower that produced these very seeds, now shelled and salted, in the palm of his hand. Oh the luxury, the pure, sensual pleasure of this human life! The smells and tastes and textures! The delightful undeniable *earthiness* of it all! He pours himself an inch of wine, swirls it around the glass and leans in for a deep, long sniff. Marvellous. He takes the smallest of sips and holds it in his mouth. Cherries and black pepper and something else, something dark and mineral. Something from a dank, cool cave deep in the woods. The wine warms his throat as he swallows it and he can feel it trail down the middle of his chest. Absolutely scrumptious.

He will eat his delicious lamb dinner and finish this entire bottle of wine, getting warmly drinky-drunk and listening to Amos's music. How he loves music! What a seemingly endless variety there is! He is determined to work his way through all of rock music, but right now he has ears only for David Bowie and Lou Reed. He loves how silly and serious and magical they are all at the same time. Sometimes he thinks they may be one person divided in two.

Except this.

David Bowie is the coolest earthling of all time. Women, men, aliens love him. As they should.

But Lou Reed knows everything. If you just listen, it is all there.

He knows that the world can be terrible and that humans struggle to find their way. That's why they need kicks.

He knows that some kicks can kill you (like heroine and brute violence) and others (like love and rock and roll) can save your life.

He knows that sometimes only the tuba can adequately express rock and roll feelings. And he knows how important it is to – how exactly does he put it? *Shake your buns*.

So, the Leader turns up the music and stands in the middle of the living room. He raises his arms above his head and shakes his hips until he can feel the meat of his buttocks shaking on the bone.

And later, when he has danced enough, when he feels he can't keep his eyes open another minute and his chin starts to sink toward his chest, he will rouse himself and stagger to the bedroom. He will take off his clothes and lay himself down on the springy mattress, his head nestled into the puffy pillow, and he will sleep the dreamy night away.

Tomorrow, he will give the crew an update.

Perhaps tomorrow.

Lit up

THE PHONE NEVER LETS HER BE.

It is Friday night and the phone is ringing as Margaret pulls on her coat and walks out the door. It keeps ringing behind the closed door as she walks down the hallway. She knows who it is. Brian calls every day now, once a day, and she never, ever answers. He always leaves a message. His tone is professional, his script unwavering. He will not sign the papers she has sent to him. Her demands are unreasonable. He has sent copies of an alternative agreement to Bob Sherman's office and to her apartment. She should look at them and they should talk. Alone. He wishes she would be realistic. He wishes they could be (and Margaret listens carefully for a catch in his throat, for the sound of him choking on his words) *friends*. He will, however, if he does not hear from her soon, take action to have the matter heard by the court. And she will lose.

Brian can huff and puff all he wants. Bob has advised her not to speak to him and not to read the papers and she will heed his good counsel. The phone goes silent abruptly, mid-ring.

Margaret heads down the stairs and onto the street. Now that she has both a roommate and a mother in her apartment she finds she needs a walk each evening. She has a system: five blocks west, five blocks north, five blocks east and five blocks south finds her back where she started. It is a good, long walk. She can stretch it to an hour if she really dawdles. In spite of the purported safety risks, she loves walking alone at night in the city, when it is quiet and beautiful and lit up. This particular circuit brings her all the things she loves best. She walks past glowing office towers, past deserted parks with paths garlanded with globes of light, past rows of houses with their TVs flashing blue, black alleys cutting back from the street. And finally on the last leg of her nightly excursion, heading home, she passes her neighbourhood shops: the grocery shop and deli, the coffee shop, the book store and the record store. On Fridays they are open late and she looks in each one, spying on the people inside.

On one person in particular, thinks the Leader.

She had only been half-surprised to see him there behind the counter, his orange hair glowing like a beacon. Clown hair. She knew she had seen him somewhere before. Now she can never go inside the record store again.

Amos looks out and sees her standing in the street and he can't believe his luck. Margaret is standing right there with her hands in her pockets looking into the window of his shop. Her cheeks are pink from the cold and her long hair shines under the streetlight. He likes these things about her; these and every other thing. He likes her purple scarf and her brown coat and her leather boots. He likes her eyes behind her glasses that will not meet his. He wants to run out but he can't leave the cash. He is working alone. He stares at her, willing her to notice him, to look his way. He waves and smiles, but it is as though the window is a one-way mirror. He swears she is looking right at him and not seeing him. He groans out loud as she turns and walks away. The night customers, the stragglers, look up from the racks of CDs briefly and return to their systematic rummaging.

Margaret hastens down the street toward home, her heart pounding. All she wants to be is inside her apartment, hidden. She wants to go inside and watch TV with Marie and Rose and shut him completely out of her mind.

Except she also wants to see him.

She wants to see him and she wants to hide from him in equal measure.

Her stomach feels queasy and her skin is clammy. What she hasn't told anyone is that she has been thinking about Amos a lot these past two weeks. These weeks that have been so strange, so unusually full of people and things to do. Secretly, she has been thinking about him just a little bit every day.

She has been thinking about the freckles on his lips.

The vestibule

THE BUZZER RINGS and it goes through Margaret like a gunshot. Rose and Marie, who are squeezed onto the couch on either side of her, turn and look at the colour draining from her face. Rose gets up and heads for the intercom by the door. "Yes?"

"Is Margaret home? It's Amos."

Rose pauses and looks at her daughter who is shrinking into the couch cushions and staring steadfastly at the television. "Yes, just a minute."

Margaret glares at her mother. She walks over to the intercom and puts her face as close to it as possible. "*Did you follow me home? Are you crazy?*"

"Margaret, I knew where you lived anyway, I saw you come here that day after the workshop, remember? Your name is on the directory down here anyway. Can I come up?"

"No way."

"Then come down here. Just for a minute."

"OK. Shut up. I'm coming." She considers not going down. She could just sit back down on the couch and ignore the buzzer for the rest of the evening. There was a time in her life, quite recently in fact, when she could have pulled this off. No one would have been the wiser. Suddenly, though, her life has an audience.

Marie and Rose are looking at her over the back of the couch. If they had tails they would be wagging. Margaret checks her look in the mirror by the door and smoothes her hair down with her hands, adjusts her posture. "I'll be right back."

She sees him before he sees her. She is coming down the stairs and she can see him standing there in the harsh yellow light of the vestibule. His hands are shoved into his jeans pockets and he is staring at his feet. He looks up and smiles as if his face will break open. Margaret tries to stop herself from smiling back, but the force is too powerful. They are grinning at each other like imbeciles by the time she opens the door and steps into the cold vestibule with him. He puts his hands on her shoulders and runs them down her arms and holds both her hands. "I am so glad to see you."

"Why?"

"I don't know. Because I thought I would never see you again, I guess." He looks at her and she is looking down and shaking her head. But she is still smiling. "What?"

"I don't know." She squeezes his hands and leans in close and puts her cheek against his. He smells like fresh air and his skin is warm. She slides her cheek along his until their lips meet and they are kissing slowly, lightly, tasting each other. He is delicious. She knew he would be. She leans against the wall and he leans in against her and they are making out full-on like teenagers. She runs her hands through his hair and over his ears and his neck. Her knees want to buckle, her body wants to sink down onto the ground and pull him on top of her.

But this is the vestibule.

She pulls back and they are smiling at each other again only now the air is thick and warm and they can barely catch their breath. "I should go back up now. You should go."

He kisses her neck and rests his palm on her cheek. "Come see me at the store. I'm always there. We can go out after I close, any night you like. Make it soon though."

She nods. "Tomorrow."

The host and the parasite

THE LEADER HAS COME UNMOORED. He is sloshing around inside Amos as he strolls home looking at the sky. And it is damn hot in there. Hot and noisy. The blood is singing. The heart is howling at the moon. The brain is a mess of shimmering chemical flashes. And the Leader can feel all of it, from the top of his curly head to the tips of his toes. Never was there a happier parasite! Never was there a happier host!

Amos is walking slowly, savouring this lingering heat in his body, this giddy lightness in his brain. He is lucky, so lucky. He knows that she will come to see him tomorrow. Thank God. What a fool he has been and how well it has served him! It all could have gone so differently. He is not sure where he had found the nerve to go to her apartment, but he is grateful for it now. Grateful and relieved, thrilled, mad with desire. Sloppy with schoolboy crush.

The aliens are watching from the ship and they are astonished. They can see their Leader in there, his glowing green-blue form inside the human. He is there and then he is gone again. The screen goes blank. The aliens fall to their knees and bow their heads. They are humbled once again by the sheer ingenuity of their Leader, the audacity. His powers are unequalled. They will spend the night in meditation, seeking understanding.

Meanwhile, Margaret is making her slow way up the stairs, trying to wipe the grin off her face before she gets to the apartment and confronts the enquiries that are surely awaiting her. The smile is so persistent and so wide that her cheeks are aching. She can't contain it for more than a moment at a time. She opens the door and Marie and Rose are still there – on the couch, tails wagging. They take in her shining, whisker-burned face and she starts laughing and she can't stop. Her glasses are smudged and slightly crooked. She is laughing so hard, she claps her hand over her mouth. Tears are streaming down her face. They continue to stare at her, eyebrows raised, but catching her smile. Rose is pleased, if unnerved. "Jesus, Margaret – sorry, Marie – are you going to tell us what's going on or what? Come sit down, you goof."

Margaret collapses between them on the couch and she is awash in affection for the two of them, these two women who have invaded her life. Her crazy mother, as usual, is infuriating and irresistible. But nothing could have prepared Margaret for how much she cares for Marie. This young woman who is really nothing like Margaret, who was at first incomprehensible to her, has become one of her very favourite people. She is fascinated by her seriousness and by her determination to be good and to do right. But more than that, Margaret knows that Marie has accepted her as her sister in spite of all her obvious shortcomings. Marie has attached herself to Margaret and will ride out whatever wave comes their way. And to Margaret's surprise, she welcomes it.

It is unspoken and true and it is gold: they are in this together.

Blossom

Rain is drumming against the window. She has been awake for most of the night listening to the rain and thinking about his face. Why does he like her so much? Is he crazy? Will he stop liking her when he knows her better? She hopes not. She likes him and desires him with a stupid certainty. She cannot shake it. It is painful to hope so much. It is painful and thrilling. Her body rejects sleep, rejects food. How will she get through this night and through the day tomorrow? The agony of waiting.

Lying there, this is the song that is going through Margaret's head: "Blossom" by James Taylor. The corniest, goofiest love song ever written. Oh, it is bad. Make no mistake. In her mind, she is flooded with seventies sunshine, white eyelet dress fluttering in the breeze, skipping through fields of flowers. *La, la, la-la-la, la, la, la, la.*

James Taylor.

She must never speak of this. Ever. Margaret remembers Rose once saying of James Taylor that he could be her 'handy man' any time. Gross.

She gets out of bed and looks out the window. Above the buildings she can see the edge of the moon shining behind black clouds. The rain is lighter now and there are patches of grey in the black sky, but no stars. She spots again the orange-pink light beside the moon. It trembles and fades and she loses sight of it. What can it possibly be? A satellite? She feels a cool hand slide onto her forehead and she collapses back onto him. She had known he would be here tonight.

The Leader holds her from behind. He knows this could be the last time he will be here in this apartment. This is the last time he will touch her smooth human skin.

She turns around to face him and studies his kind eyes, the shining skin on the dome of his head. He walks her to the middle of the room and kneels down on the floor. Margaret kneels, too, facing him. This reminds Margaret of being a child, of sharing a secret. Their foreheads are touching. The Leader takes her hands and opens them up like a book, places them palm-up on his knees.

He pushes one green thumb into the middle of her right hand, like he is pushing a button. Like he is *rebooting* her. He looks at her to see if she understands. She does not. She only knows that she does not want him to leave, she is not ready. How simple it is to be in this dream world with him. How easy. He loves her and she doesn't care why. She just wants him to stay, for the dream to ramble on, just slowly play out its weird story forever. Ordinary life is too hard. Margaret lays her head on the Leader's smooth shoulder.

Gently, he raises her up and turns her toward the window again. He stands up straight, winks at her, and before her saucer eyes he rises off the floor and slowly draws his knees up to his chest – he is a shining ball, suspended in mid-air – and disappears.

Margaret is astonished to see the giant orange-pink orb hovering outside her window. Ten stories high. It is made of steel and blinking lights dot its circumference. It hangs there, twinkling like an enormous Christmas ornament. She feels she could reach out and touch it – it is that close and that real. The streetlights dim and quiver. The orb turns liquidy gold and blurs around the edges. It pulses twice and vanishes into the night.

Closing time

The record store is always irritatingly busy at closing time, especially on Saturdays. Not for the first time, Amos surveys his clientele, noting how it grows older and more male with every passing year. There was a time when the record store was the domain of youth. Not so these days. The young and the cool are at home downloading digital tracks onto pods. These days the record store is the haunt of adult nerds like Amos. Of men who wander the streets alone on Saturdays not entirely sure what to do with themselves. Except they are eager to demonstrate how much they know about Black Flag or The Grateful Dead or – God help him – Rush, because if it is Rush they will never stop talking, and will not go home until told to do so, gently, several times. And there are the men that have been banished from the house by their women – sometimes alone, sometimes pushing a stroller. And sometimes, though rarely now, the customer is a former sullen punk rock girl grown into a sullen bewitching woman like Margaret. A woman who will sneer openly at the selection of CDs you have so painstakingly put together for her, but will launch into an ode to a new record she has found with the zeal of a preacher.

And if you know anything about what she is saying, if you agree with her, she will stay and talk to you.

Her eyes will light up and she will snicker with you like a guy.

A dream girl.

The dream girl

"I might not be home tonight. Don't wait up."

Margaret rubs at the sliver in the palm of her hand with her thumb. She puts her gloves on and grabs her purse. She is trying for nonchalance and not quite hitting the mark. Her voice is off-key. She sounds like someone else. Someone completely fucking crazy.

"Really," says Rose.

Marie does not dare say a word.

"Really. Wish me luck!" And she is out the door. Each step down the stairs, each step down the street is an effort. Her feet are mud. She is pushed and pulled on the inside. She is dying to see him and she is scared to death. She is in the twilight zone now, a new strange world she could not have imagined. As a married person, Margaret had presumed that she would never again kiss someone for the first time and after her marriage had ended, she had not really adjusted this view. And now it has happened. New lips have touched her own. It was magic, a miracle. More sobering than this, she has not shown her naked body to someone new in more than a decade. To be honest, she doesn't even like to look at it herself.

She puts one mud foot in front of the other until she is there in front of the store a full twenty minutes early. Christ. She walks briskly past the door and goes to the grocery store where she wanders the aisles for an interminable five minutes and finally buys some gum. She stands around on the sidewalk chewing until she is chilled to the bone. She spits out her gum and heads back to the record store. Her nose is running now. Perfect.

Amos had seen her walk by earlier and wondered where in the hell she was going. He is profoundly relieved to see her now, coming through the door. He takes her coat and offers her his stool behind the cash and unceremoniously shoos his lingering customers out the door, muttering apologies and locking the door behind them. He nervously sets about the dozen or so small tasks he must complete in order to close the store for the night – there are calculations to be made, switches to be switched, things to be shifted from one place to another. It is very quiet in the store now and he can feel her vibrating on top of the stool, emitting waves of anxiety. "You know what I like about you Margaret?"

"What?"

"Everything." He walks over to her and kisses her forehead, each of her eyelids, her mouth, sweet and wet as a plum. "Let's get out of here. I think a drink is in order."

Margaret lowers herself carefully off the stool, fearing she will catch a foot on a rung and crash to the floor. She takes his hand and they make their way through the darkened store. She stands perfectly still by the door as he sets the alarm and they are released into the cold night, bolting for the nearest bar.

Taking it all off

THE BOOTH IS WARM and the beer is cold and they are sitting unreasonably close to each other. If nothing good ever happens to her again she will remember the heat of his leg against hers. She will remember the frightening flush in her face, the rush of blood in her ears, the divine ache between her legs. (Thank God, it lives!) She will remember his smile, his hands, his careful flattery. Margaret looks around and imprints the details of this place on her brain: the faded upholstery, the dark wood, the dirty floor. She closes her eyes and lets herself savour the giant swell of pure happiness in her chest.

"Can we go to your place?" It is out of her mouth before she knows she is saying it and she feels the world stop – one, two, three, four seconds pass and she is not sure he has heard her but then he is fumbling for money to leave on the table and they are up and out of the booth and onto the street again. They are leaned against a wall, kissing, then in a cab even though he only lives six blocks away, the ride swerving and abruptly over.

The light inside Amos's building is too bright and when they get inside his apartment, they don't turn on the lights but shed their coats and their scarves and their gloves as they blunder toward the couch and they are finally touching each other's skin, the soft, hot skin that is hidden under their clothes. Their hands are sliding up shirts and down pants and their kiss is continuous, unbroken, luscious. They are tugging and pulling and unbuttoning and every piece of clothing is a maddening obstacle.

He takes her hand and leads her away from the couch, toward the bedroom. Margaret tumbles forward, tugging at her shirt to cover her pudgy white belly. Her jeans are open and the buckle of her belt is rebounding off of her left thigh as she follows him down the hallway. She is recovering her wits now and is starting to get nervous again. She is starting to lose her courage. But then something happens.

As she watches Amos walk shirtless down the hallway in front of her, something is happening to his skin. In the darkness of his apartment his pale skin looks blue and she can see a shimmering wave of green light travelling in pulses like lightning across his back. Margaret stops dead and tugs on his hand. He turns to look at her and she puts her hands on his shoulders and turns him back around. She places a hand between his shoulder blades to tell him to stay that way and then this is what she does.

Margaret H. Atwood takes off her shirt and lets it drop on the ground.

She struggles out of her very tight minimizing bra and lets her big, soft breasts loose. Amos, still looking away, can feel the hair standing up on his arms. He wants to see. He wants to turn around and pull her close, but he doesn't.

He waits in the dark at the threshold of his bedroom, listening to her undress behind him.

She rolls her pants over her hips and down to the ground and steps out of them.

One sock off and then the other.

Then (as the aliens swoon and the ship lights up in the night sky) she presses her beautiful, naked thirty-five-year-old self against his warm back and holds on for dear life.

Seven

And everyone has a shred of hope

EVERYONE, EVERYONE, EVERYONE. Everyone who isn't already dead has a shred of hope. Mothers, fathers, brothers, sisters. Aunts, uncles, cousins. Every miserable one.

All the bitches and bastards who visit terrible things upon others.

All the monsters and their victims, all the oppressors and oppressed.

All the loners and cynics.

Those who carp and moan and those who fret and stew.

The nail-biters and hair-pullers and regurgitators.

The hungry and abandoned and sick.

The homeless, the hopeless and the unloved.

All of them, all of them, all of them have a small, unreasonable, unkillable shred of hope. It is always there, just waiting to explode into happiness.

And surely it might never happen.

It may lay there dormant throughout a miserable life until it ends with a miserable death.

But it exists.

It is there in every living human.

Otherwise the aliens would be bored out of their minds.

Rose

THE DISHES, THE DISHES. Still in her house coat Rose clears the breakfast dishes from the table now that Margaret and Marie have left for work. A woman could tire of this. One month. One full month Rose has been here. For one month she has observed her daughter in her lair and finally, she is beginning to like what she sees. And as an unanticipated windfall she has revelled in the weekday solitude of Margaret's apartment. How lovely it has been to have the place to herself during the working day, even with the dishes. She has taken long, hot baths in the middle of the day, soaking until she is dizzy. She has spent a significant amount of time striding around the apartment in the nude. She has rifled through every drawer, every shelf, every nook and cranny. She has gathered as much information as possible and she is ready to report back to HQ.

Her flight is booked for tomorrow afternoon.

Dishes done, she wipes the counters and table, rinses the cloth and hangs it over the faucet. She lights a joint and pads on bare feet to her daughter's bedroom and sits down on the bed. She lays her head on Margaret's pillow and breathes in the smell of her hair, her shampoo, her laundry detergent. To Rose, Margaret's room is like a stage set. There is something about it that does not quite make sense to her. She feels like she is dreaming when she is in this room. The wonder of this creature, her daughter! This person made from the tissue and blood of her own body, now on the loose in the world with a bedroom, an apartment, a job. It defies understanding.

Rose slides open the drawers of the dresser, one by one. What she loves the most is the top drawer which is filled with underwear that is folded. Folded! Row upon row of little, identical lace soldiers lined up for battle. Undeniably, this impulse comes from Margaret's father. She thinks of the backyard shed at home where Ron has rows of hooks upon which he hangs his tools. He has drawn the outline of each tool on the wall with a Magic Marker so that when one is missing, its shadow is there, a reminder that a member of the tool family is at large and must be returned. When she had seen him doing it, drawing those outlines, Rose thought it unwise, that the system could not possibly stand. What if, for example, you lost your shears and bought new ones that were slightly larger and couldn't fit into the outline? Then what? But she should have known. More than a decade has passed and Ron's perfectly clean tools continue to hang in their assigned spots on the shed wall. Not one has ever been left behind.

Perfect Ron who has been so kind to her, who has made her life so pleasant. What stupid, blind luck to have found him. She believes firmly that she could have just as easily chosen someone completely unsuitable, a bristling thorn of a person. But what bounty: thirty-seven years of adventures, of kisses, of quiet evenings, of inside jokes. What a privilege to know another person so well and to continue to like what you find. She strives to deserve it.

Rose extinguishes her joint in the moist earth of the potted plant on Margaret's dresser and makes a mental note to retrieve it later. She carefully pushes all the drawers in, smoothes out the bedspread. She will take a quick look around Marie's room and then she will get ready to go. She wants to get a look at this Amos character before she goes home.

Amos

THEY ARE WATCHING EACH OTHER covertly. She is unconvincingly browsing through the pop music section, flipping through CDs, moving from row to row. He is casting sidelong glances at her while ringing in purchases at the cash. He had identified her immediately. Contrary to her own view of herself, she is no secret agent. Her posture, her eyes, her gait are pure Margaret; this is obviously the tree from which that superb apple fell. In some ways, Amos likes that she is here. He appreciates the opportunity to lay eyes on her and he likes it that she cares enough to come check him out. Besides, he feels up to the scrutiny these days. He is feeling exceptionally fine.

Oh, Amos. In his time, he has been called Aimless and, less charitably, *Anus*. It is true. He has suffered the running critique of his family and friends his whole life and he has suffered it gladly because he has always known that he was on the right path, the path to contentment. And look at him now! The woman he wanted, the woman he surely created with his own mind, who has now become flesh through his tireless wishing, this woman loves him. There is no denying it. Her eyes shine when she looks at him. She laughs at his jokes. She falls into his arms over and over again. And there is nothing so far as he can tell in this material world that should prevent them from being happy. They are healthy and able. They have enough money to buy the things they need. He refuses to foresee trouble, to doubt his luck. He feels like a prince, like a king surveying his land. His heart is as fat and juicy as a watermelon.

So bring on the mother-in-law.

Bring on the gripers and chronic goods-returners.

Bring on the Rush fans, bless their rock and roll hearts. Bring on the endless heralds of the collapse of the music industry as we know it, for today none of it matters. Today nothing can make a dent in the shiny, shiny chrome of his good mood.

She is staring at him openly now, she can't help it. That smile!

How can anyone smile so hard and for so long? He is a human sunbeam. She heads for the back of the checkout line and waits her turn, with no merchandise in hand. When she is finally standing before him she prepares to take her leap, to make her pitch. She knows she should mind her own business but she can't help herself. "Amos, you know who I am, right?"

"It's nice to meet you, Rose." She could eat him, he is so lovely. She looks behind her to see if there are any impatient consumers waiting in line. There are none. She is not sure how he is making a living at this racket, but will give him the benefit of the doubt for the moment.

"I'm going home tomorrow and I just wanted to meet you before I left." She wants to say that she hopes that he will make Margaret happy, even for a short time, but she can't do it. That would be going too far. She wants to say, "I hope you aren't a bastard like the last one. Please, be good. Be worthy." But none of this makes it out of her head and into the air between them. Instead she says, "It could be a while before I visit again, but I hope I will see you again. When we have more time to get to know each other."

"You will. You'll see me again, Rose. Have a good trip home."

She likes the confidence of this, the commitment. It seems right. Better not to prolong the interview and risk hearing something she likes less. Rose smiles and nods, raises a hand to say goodbye and holds her tongue. Amos watches her go and as the door swings closed behind her he thinks about her plane taking off tomorrow, about the giant vaulting arc it will follow through the sky, from east to west, and for the hundredth time this week he remembers a fortune cookie message he had recently.

It said, "Your future is as boundless as the lofty sky."

Marie

It is 10:00 a.m. Marie is at her desk and she feels certain that everything is as it should be. She has briefed Lenny on her work for the week; she has made all of her morning calls. Her tasks for the day have been enumerated and prioritized. Her heart is as light as air today because last night she was blessed with a vision. For a full week she has devoted herself to prayer. Every morning and every night she knelt until her knees were sore, her mind wide open as a windy field, waiting for direction, begging for peace of mind, and it has come.

Last night, she had been kneeling, her elbows resting on her bed in Margaret's guest room, and she had felt it. Before she even saw him, she knew he was there. The room had gone cold and still and she had felt his breath on the back of her neck. There was the scent of lilacs. When she turned she could see his shining robes and his gentle smile and then she felt his hand on her burning, tear-stained face. She can still feel the imprint of it on her cheek.

And now everything has been utterly transformed: she sees the path before her for a thousand miles. She just needs to keep walking.

It's like this. As she works, she can feel her feet on the ground, feel the files in her hands, but she can also see herself from a great height. She can see the building from the sky. She can see through the building to the spot where she stands on the ninth floor.

She can pan out and see that around the city is a halo of forest and farm fields laced with fences and paths and roads. And she knows that above the building she is standing in, above the clouds, is the great soaring endlessness of heaven.

Marie knows now that nothing, no little thing in this measly earthly existence will deter her from her mission: she will continue to tell the truth about Tom Francis no matter how difficult it is and no matter how long it takes. She will not betray the other brave girls who have stepped into the light with their sadness and shame. She will repay the kindness of those who support her and she will forgive those who don't.

She will walk the surface of the planet with the Holy Spirit howling through her heart like the wind.

Tom Francis

OH, HE KNOWS.

He knows what he is and what he has done. And he knows what he is left with, which is exactly nothing. There is not one person on the crust of this earth who cares for him, who will come to his aid. He is unforgiveable and unforgiven. He has betrayed the sacred trust of children and parents. He has used people for his own selfish pleasure at their immeasurable expense. *Pleasure.* Tom thinks that what he has felt has never been uncomplicated enough to be called pleasure. It has never been free of the terrible realization of the ugly depth of his wrongness.

And yet he had persisted

He had continued because it had been thrilling like a crazy dream. And he had continued because it had been easy. Over and over again the little girls trusted him and their parents had left them in his care. The beautiful little girls left in the care of Tom Francis, the hideous monster.

So here he is in a cage with the other monsters. And it is pretty much downhill from here. He can see the future that he will be marched though – witnesses lined up against him, a judge and jury ready to make the call. There will be no escape hatch, no clemency. Only the reckoning. So he has made a decision. From now on, he will only say yes. To every accusation, he will say yes.

Yes it was me.

Yes I am guilty.

Because it is true and because it will be over faster. And maybe this way he will not have to look at their faces. And maybe they will not have to look at his.

He will be thrown back in a cell and he will withstand the drip, drip, drip of time and one day he will be released. They will not keep him there forever. And when it is over, when he has spent hundreds and hundreds of nights thinking about what he has done, when he steps into the world again where no one will welcome him, where no one will say his name, will something have changed? Will the black, dry husk of his callous heart be transformed? Is there anything else in there but black, bitter coal? Is there anything of any use to anyone? He doesn't know. It is too soon to tell. He knows that the most he can hope for is very little indeed.

And he will go ahead and hope for it anyway.

Ron

HE AWAITS HER RETURN. Here in this hard chair by the window, squinting into the blinding sunlight, Ron watches planes taxi to and fro and he waits for the one that will carry her back to him where she belongs. She has been gone for weeks now and when she is gone he wants her back. He wants her somewhere around him, within reach. He has had this feeling since the very first day they met and it persists, undiminished. It is not that he is helpless without her or that he is terribly lonely. It is just that, given the choice, he would just always rather have her with him than not. She makes him laugh. And he sleeps better. This time especially his sleep has been strange in her absence – fitful, hallucinatory. Each night has been filled with periods where he can't be sure if he is asleep or awake. The surroundings seem familiar, but something is distinctly off, askew. There is a buzzing in the air, a weird energy. Many nights he has lain on his back, his heart pounding, wondering if he is in the right bed.

Even so, he has not foregone the privileges of temporary bachelorhood: he has had his share of tuna sandwich dinners while seated in front of the television, wearing only his bathrobe; he has not once, in an entire month, closed the bathroom door. He has systematically rearranged items in every room so they are just the way he likes them. He has alphabetized books as well as jars of spices. He has cleared every surface of clutter – counters, dresser tops, the top of the fridge, all are gleaming shiny expanses like ice rinks. He has thrown out every expired or mostly empty bottle, jar or box in every cupboard and cabinet. The peace this brings him is profound. And yet all these are pleasures halved without someone to thwart him at every turn.

Then somewhere out of his sight, the great silver bird descends from the clear, bright, blue sky, filled with its fleshy cargo. Two hundred passengers, crammed together, hearts beating more or less steadily in the birdcages of their chests. They are chewing gum and sweating in their rumpled clothes as the landing gear strains for the ground and the plane bumps once, twice and hurtles to a dead stop. Those who were holding their breath release it. The murmur of conversation replaces the roar of the engines. Newspapers are folded, phones switched on, seatbelts are removed in defiance of the admonitions of the flight attendants and the dozens of tiny lit up signs.

Ron spots the plane angling slowly toward the gate and he is on his feet. A full ten minutes will pass before he sees her familiar shape coming through the doorway, her great big smile. He will stand until then. He will stand and watch until she comes through the door and walks toward him and he will let the bliss of her return fill him from the feet up.

Lenny

LENNY HAS MADE UP HIS MIND. It is all coming together in his head now. He is going off the rails.

He can see what will happen next. He can't believe it has taken him so long to see it, to put the plan in motion. He puts his cutlery down on the table and walks away; he will not clear the table tonight or wash the dishes. He will never again wash the dishes in this house or mop the floors or clean the toilet. All of that is over now. Finished. His wife and daughters stare after him as he walks down the hallway and pads up the stairs. They can hear him running a bath up there. Again.

Lenny has not spoken to his family for two weeks now. Not a single word. His resolve has been unshakeable. It had started one evening, a night like many others, when he had been sitting at the dinner table with Sharlene, Becky and Lisa. He had started to say something, to ask them a question about something, just to make conversation and he had, as usual, been interrupted. When he tried again to speak, he had been mocked and insulted. On his third attempt, a Brussels sprout had bounced off his temple, launched with a fork by Lisa, his youngest daughter.

Lenny's life had suddenly snapped into focus.

A switch had been flipped, a decision had been made for him by a higher power.

He felt released, relieved of a crushing burden. He would no longer leak words into the air for the entertainment of these people. There would be no more trying. No more trying to charm them, to win their favour. No more wheedling for sex with his wife. He had wiped the butter off his face with his napkin and pushed his chair back from the table. He picked up one of the family's three cats, pressed his face into its soft fur and walked away.

And now, two weeks later, they are down there surrounded by piles of dirty dishes and he is up here in his oasis. The door is locked and the fan is running so he can't really hear them. He has stuffed a facecloth into the overflow drain and filled the tub to the very brim with scalding hot water. His skin is lobster red. He slides down low, rests his head against the wall, puts his feet up on the edge of the tub. He will stay until the water gets cold and even then he won't get out. He will pull the plug and let the water drain around him, feeling gravity slowly returning his body weight to the bottom of the tub. Then he will get up, put on his bathrobe and go to his bed. But he won't sleep.

Not tonight.

He will wait for Sharlene to lumber into the room and collapse onto the bed beside him. He will wait until she begins to snore and then he will steal away in the middle of the night. He will steal away and he will never come back to this house. His bag is packed and in the trunk of the car. His new, empty apartment is waiting for him downtown. The keys have been hanging on the rack by the front door in full view of anyone who might give a damn, glowing like a beacon, for days.

Brian

BIG BAD BRIAN, THERE HE IS, sitting on the couch on a Saturday morning, his hand resting on his belly, watching golf on TV and looking perfectly ordinary.

Hardly the romantic villain at all.

Sandie is in the kitchen clattering around as usual and all is well, or at least it should be. But today there is something nagging at Brian. In fact everything is nagging at him. For example, he doesn't like the way his belly is getting soft, puffing out like a marshmallow over the waist of his trousers. Also, he has the feeling that he is wasting his Saturday, that he should be doing something more fun, more interesting. Maybe he has stalled in his career – will they ever make him a partner? He feels his hair is getting thin, that his jackets don't fit right. He thinks that Sandie is starting to look tired and old around her eyes and he is pretty certain that he detects a note of sarcasm in her voice when she speaks to him. She doesn't seem to laugh quite so readily at his jokes these days. Does he imagine these things?

Flies, gnats, grains of sand. He feels them he swears. Sand in his eyes, in his shirt. Tiny insects in his nose, in his brain. A constant physical annoyance. He can't sit still, always brushing at his nose, scratching at his armpits, tugging at his clothing. *Everything is bothering him*. Poor old, goat-footed Brian. What can the matter be? He thinks maybe it is the way the weather is getting colder, the way the days are getting shorter. He has always hated this time of year, the way the light dies like a door slowly closing.

Maybe he should book a trip with one of his friends. Or maybe he should go alone. Somewhere warmer and more hospitable. Some climate where women wear less clothing and don't know him quite so well.

He has been watching the golfers tee off, the balls soaring through the blue sky, the hushed crowds clustered around the emerald carpets of the greens. But he keeps fading out. He is having trouble paying attention. He is distracted by his own thoughts, a litany of irritations, insecurities, problems. Margaret. Especially her. Why, God, oh why had he ever married? He is clearly not suited for marriage. What a mess! What an expense! And for what? A sham. Guilt every day for ten years. He has been found guilty and will pay an enormous fine. The divorce. It is a game of chicken, now. The truth is that Brian doesn't really stand a chance. He is bluffing. He is a nude emperor. A court will find in her favour and he will find himself paying for that, too.

So what? Does he cry uncle and sign the papers? Maybe. But, not yet. He will make her wait some more, a few more weeks, maybe a couple of months. What's the hurry? Brian stretches his legs and rests his slippered feet on top of the coffee table. Maybe he is starting to feel a little bit better, a little bit calmer. *Women*. What torment! His whole life he has wanted them and for his whole life he has hated them for making him want them. He needs to rethink the whole thing. He certainly has to stop bringing them into his home. Women are so much nicer, so much prettier when they don't live in your house! In your house they take on smells, they age. They cannot stop telling you what they think.

In the precise way she does every morning, Sandie takes the dishes out of the dishwasher and stacks them one by one on the shelves. She hates these fucking dishes with their stupid geometric patterns, so tacky as to be comical. Margaret's dishes: another woman's dishes in another woman's kitchen. Sandie's stomach feels tight and bloated. Her armpits smell sour and a giant tuberous pimple is pushing its painful way to the surface of the skin on her chin. It is the sexiest time of the month again and she is feeling the timeless rage of being a woman.

In the other room the sultan lounges on the couch watching television. With her elbow she nudges an ugly coffee cup off the counter and it smashes to pieces on the ceramic tile. "One down," she thinks, "nine to go!" In the living room Brian furrows his brow.

"Everything OK in there?" Jesus.

"Not really, no." She says this quietly enough that he can't quite catch it. He listens for a moment and then turns his attention back to the television. There will be no dishes left at all at this rate.

Brushing the shards into the dustpan, Sandie wonders as she does every month on the day before her period begins, why she loves him, why she continues to live in this house. There was a time when he was entertaining and she was able to disregard his cold-bloodedness, his many betrayals. There was a time when she could convince herself that it was all worth it. Now, he is less charming, less funny. Frankly, he is less attractive. And yet (and this is the most humiliating part of the whole thing) she continues to hope, to yearn for his approval. She has continued to dream, like a lovesick teenager, that he will fall to one knee and propose marriage. Another fool in the chain, chain, chain. And she knows. She knows that soon he is going to leave her and he will be doing her a favour.

Brian is up off the couch and out the door, head held high, change jingling in his pocket. He is on his way to the travel agent where he will book his two-week vacation. He will call Sandie from his hotel and tell her to pack up, to move along. He will tell her that they both know it is wrong, that it is ridiculous to continue. He will get out while the gettin's good and then he will downsize severely: a bachelor apartment with one dresser, one closet, one set of keys, and he will do his best to keep things simple from now on.

Margaret

SHE KNOWS ALREADY, she can feel it. She knows by the way the blood sings in her ears, by the way her breakfast feels like it is in her chest instead of in her belly. She can tell by the way she has been sleeping, so deep and immobile. She seems to wake up in the exact position she started in, her pillow crushed with the weight of her head, creases on her face. Each morning she has to peel her one reddened ear off the side of her head.

Night, which was once a biathlon event of bedclothes wrestling and corridor pacing, has become an eight-hour patch of lost time – one long blink of the eye.

She knows already but she will not jinx it by thinking about it too much. She can wait. She is feeling entirely unruffled.

The Leader (what Margaret remembers)

MARGARET HAS THE SAME DREAM every night. It is only a dream. Maybe it is the stupidest dream anyone has ever had. And yet she remembers every second of it, every silly frame. One minute she is lying in bed, sweltering under the quilts in the dead of winter, fat and wide and ungainly as a manatee. The next minute, it begins.

She opens her eyes and it is summertime. She is on the white horse, thundering through the green valley and she can hear the thumping of the hooves on the ground, the rush of the wind through her hair, the swish of the tall grass beneath them as they fly along. The muscles of the horse's back are churning beneath her. Through the valley, up onto the crest of a hill.

"*Whoa, Nelly!*"

Margaret stops to survey her land. The horse shuddering and snorting, shifting from hoof to hoof. Fields and fields of purple clover as far as the eye can see. All hers. She dismounts and walks the horse down the hill, letting the reins drop from her hand as they reach the bottom. The sun is glittering, brilliant. Everything has been dipped in honey. Margaret can feel the warm, moist earth on her bare feet as she sets out across the field. The clover is teeming with fat bees, making their lazy way from blossom to blossom. The field is a carpet of bees, a chorus of buzzing bees, droning like bag pipes.

Not one will sting her.

They wouldn't dare.

She owns this joint.

She looks up at the blue sky and there, on a cloud, in lotus position is Prince. The man himself. Guitar cradled in his lap, lavender shirt open to the navel, rippling in the wind. Cherubs fluttering around his head. She nods. He nods back. Under her feet, she feels the single massive thud of the yogi's heartbeat. Her own heart is still and quiet, suspended in the liquid beauty of the magical dreamworld she has made. It will not beat again until she is awake.

Then it will race.

At the horizon she can see a figure. She has had this dream many times before, so she knows who it is. It is the green man. From here, though, at this point in the dream, he is only a black dot between the purple of the field and the blue of the sky.

She keeps walking.

A cloud passes over the sun and the field is in shadow. Margaret stumbles over an ugly brown suitcase that is suddenly there, in her way. She knows that suitcase. How did it get here? She kneels down on the ground and fumbles to find the tab of the zipper and quickly, like ripping off a Band-Aid, she runs it around the front of the suitcase, letting it fly open like a jack-in-the-box. She stands up and backs away. Then it happens.

A bright orange kite rises up, swaying like a snake, out of the suitcase and up into the sky, ribbons trailing behind it one hundred feet long. The cloud is swept away from the face of the sun, carried away with the kite and the light pours down once again on Margaret's kingdom.

He is closer now.

The Leader stands tall. Seven feet tall. His suit is dove grey, pin-striped, perfectly tailored. He wears a crisp white shirt and a yellow polka-dot tie. His briefcase is black. He feels good. He feels like the Lord Himself as the sun shines down on him. His feet hover just a little above the warm, moist surface of the earth as he walks toward her.

He walks until he is right in front her. Towering. The bees sing, a chorus of miniature angels.

He takes her hands in his. With his long, green fingers, he turns them over and back. Smooth and perfect. No marks, no scaly patches. He kneels down to examine her bare feet. Also perfect. She smiles down at him, smoothing her white eyelet dress over her thighs. He wraps his arms around her waist, rests his head between her breasts. Just for a minute. He wants to feel this so he can remember it. And he wants one other thing, too.

The alien stands again, brushes off the pants of his fine summer-weight wool suit. He picks up his briefcase and takes Margaret by the hand, leading her to the shade beneath a tree at the edge of the field. The horse, who has been delicately tugging clumps of clover out of the ground with his teeth, stands up, chewing, and looks toward the couple. The Leader sweeps his arm toward the ground and Margaret sits. He sits, too, lays his briefcase across his lap and releases the catches.

(He loves the sound they make when they open and he loves the sound they make when they close. He could open and close his briefcase all day long, just for the sheer pleasure of hearing the sound.)

From the briefcase he produces a book. It is a hardcover, dust jacket long gone, cream coloured with a maroon spine. The gold lettering says: **Atwood The Handmaid's Tale**. He turns the book over in his hand, flips to the title page and hands it to her, along with a pen.

She looks at him. He makes a waving motion with his hand and nods his head. She shakes her head. No. He has it wrong. Doesn't he know? (Of course, he knows!) The alien takes the pen and puts it in her right hand and lowers the tip until it touches the page. He looks from her to the page, from the page to her, and then nods again. He lets go of her hand.

"For James," he says. Donald Sutherland, all the way. Excellent. He nods again.

James? She is skeptical. But she does it anyway.

In black ink, she writes: *For James – best wishes – Margaret H. Atwood*.

He takes the book away and stashes it in his briefcase, which he latches with a decisive *clunk*. And he kisses her right on the mouth.

The gates

IT IS SUNDAY MORNING, star date February 13, 2005. The sun is shining and the crows outside are screaming. Perhaps to them, as interpreted by the tiny earholes in their shiny black heads, it is singing. Perhaps it is just some friendly conversation, but to Margaret it sounds like a cycle of blood-curdling screams.

Amos is at work and Marie is at church, so apart from the chorus of crows, Margaret has been left in peace to enjoy a lazy, solitary morning: she is still in her pyjamas, she has just brewed a fresh pot of tea and the newspaper awaits her on the kitchen table. She smoothes out the front section and is greeted by a front page, the likes of which she has never seen. In a large photo in the centre of the page there are banners of brilliant yellow-orange against the stark grey winter landscape of Central Park and there are hordes of people, all of them smiling. The headline reads, "In a Saffron Ribbon, A Billowy Gift to the City." Margaret cannot imagine what this could possibly mean, but clearly something spectacular is happening in New York City, something that has never happened before.

The aliens know what it is. They have been following its progress for decades; they have been stationed above Central Park for months now, watching as the thousands of steel frames were erected one by one along the winding foot paths; watching as over 165,000 steel bolts were fitted into place. They cheered yesterday when the panels of saffron fabric were set free to flutter in the breeze. Hooray for Christo and Jeanne-Claude! Three cheers for Mayor Bloomberg! They watched in silent reverence as the artists toured their creation. They followed the slow progress of the limousine as it threaded its way in and out of the trees along the more than twenty miles of foot path, the gates looking like a giant trail of dominoes, ready to be nudged into a chain reaction.

What a perfect day: a river of people walking through the gates, watching the new curtains ruffle in the wind above their heads, the sunlight shining through them. The aliens can feel the way the human hearts lighten inside their chests, how they bubble up in wonder. Chins are lifted. Faces are turned toward the sky instead of the earth, instead of toward their shoes. Children are lifted onto shoulders to take a swipe at the fabric.

It is a fabulous tangerine parade.

Margaret is riveted. She reads the front page story, examines each photograph. She counts. There are no less than fifteen pieces in the newspaper on this event: historical features with timelines, editorials, biographies of the artists, interviews with volunteers. She reads every word of every article while her tea goes cold and bitter in the pot and the crows flap noisily up into the air, over the rooftops and west to the park where they settle in the trees.

This crazy thing, this twenty-six-year effort, has taken place entirely without Margaret's knowledge. She struggles to understand it. How does such a thing happen? How do two people – apparently without sponsorship or donations – raise over twenty-one million dollars? How, *why* do these same people spend days, nights, months, years developing a NASA-worthy plan, including hundreds (thousands?) of drawings and studies and projections? What force within them enables them to spend MORE THAN TWENTY YEARS OF THEIR LIVES trying to sell their idea to any number of unreceptive city councils and committees, and when they finally prevail, hire or cajole thousands of workers, oversee the manufacturing and installation of seven thousand five hundred gates of steel and fabric along the maze of footpaths of Central Park?

How?

Seven thousand five hundred steel frames constructed, one million square feet of yellow-orange fabric cut and pleated, forty-six miles of hems sewn! How many human hours? How many days and nights? It is staggering.

But there is something more baffling even than this: at the end of sixteen days, a small army of workers will return to the park and take it all down. All of it. No tree or shrub will have been disturbed. No hole in the earth will be left to attest to its existence. It will be gone as if it were never there, swept away. A mirage, a vision. A million sets of memories imprinted on a million human brains. More than that: millions upon millions. It will be a story that gets told over and over again: once, for only sixteen days, there were thousands of brilliant, fluttering gates in Central Park. But, only once. Never since and never again.

The aliens know.
    Only humans would ever do such a thing.
    Only humans could dream it; only humans could come together and make it. And only humans could truly appreciate it once it was there.
    Because it helps them forget about their suffering.
    And it reminds them that they have magical powers.
    They are the only creatures in the universe capable of forgetting.

Margaret makes a decision to go to New York City. She will make the pilgrimage. She will go and she will take Amos with her and together they will look at every gate, from one to seven thousand five hundred. They will walk the wandering paths of the park and they will look at each one and something will happen to them, something will change. She is certain of it. She can see it in the face of every person in that picture on the front page. Their eyes are shining. The adults look like children, radiant and giddy; the children look like adults, grave and reverent. These gates are a magic tunnel, a portal to another consciousness. It is a channel of peace.
    They will enter it together and they will exit it together.
    Amen.

Epilogue

The pain is blinding. She is shaking so hard that the bed clatters against the wall. Her mother is holding one of her feet and Amos is holding the other and she is pushing with all her might. Her face is as red as a beet. Warm water is seeping out of her and soaking everything. Someone is telling her to "push deeper, push in your *bottom*" and then, abruptly, she is told to stop. She listens to the thud of her heart for a minute and the rush of pain starts again, it is like an electric shock running the length of her spine. She pushes harder this time, harder and longer.

The doctor, who is between her legs, raises his hand, tells her to hold on, the baby is coming. Her vagina is a raw burning halo. She reaches down and feels the top of the baby's head and starts to cry. The desire to push is satanic. It is like the ocean is inside her and it wants to come out. She is grunting.

"Push!" says the doctor, and she is folding in half, grinding down like a bulldozer. Suddenly, like a cork from a bottle the baby's head is out and they tell her to stop again. She is moaning like an animal, like the animal she is. Her mother is grinning like a moron, tears spilling down her cheeks. The doctor shoves something up the baby's nose to clear it. He feels around its neck to make sure the cord is not there. The bed is shaking and Margaret arches in pain. She pushes without being told to and as though she is being turned inside out, being torn wide open, the baby is out. It is raised high, a slippery fish, a bright blue cord twisting out of his belly, leading back inside her. Cheers go up.

A boy! Amos has his hand over his mouth. He cannot stop laughing, is dancing from foot to foot. Rose is hugging everyone within reach.

The cord is cut and the baby is taken to a table where nurses are rubbing him and wrapping him and writing things down. Margaret cannot take her eyes off of him. She wants to hold him. She wants to smell him; she wants to *breathe him in*. But her body is still at work, still carrying out its plan. There is a wave of pain, a pressing down and she is pushing again. The placenta slithers out, a fat blood pudding. The doctor examines it and proclaims it whole. He shows it to Margaret who doesn't really care to see it. Finally, finally, the baby is handed to her, tightly wrapped in a soft pale green blanket. He is wearing an unimaginably small yellow knitted hat. She lays her hot cheek against his tiny face and feels his breath. Such small puffs of breath, barely there. She looks at him and he makes a squawk and looks back at her.

He is perfect.

His eyes are steely dark blue and lovely.

They are blue like the planet earth from space.

Acknowledgements

Information from the following *New York Times* articles was relied upon in the writing of this book to demonstrate the hopelessness and wonder of the human world:

Lillian and Julia: A Twilight of Fear by N.R. Kleinfield, December 12, 2004

Farewell, Africa: Beggar, Serf, Soldier, Child by Somini Sengupta, December 12, 2004

Who's Preying on Your Grandparents? Selling Annuities to Investors Who May Not Outlive Them by Gretchen Morgenson, May 15, 2005

In a Saffron Ribbon, A Billowy Gift to the City by Michael Kimmelman, February 13, 2005

Dressing the Park in Orange, and Pleats by James Barron, February 13, 2005

Margaret's painting, described on page 96, is *St. James the Greater*, Giovanni Battista Tiepolo, 1749.